NEW ORLEANS GO CUP CHRONICLES

Rescued by A Kiss

Dead and Breakfast

Drive Thru Murder

Death By Rum Balls

Dog Gone & Dead

Politicians, Potholes & Pralines

DEATH by RUM BALLS
BOOK 4 in The New Orleans Go Cup Chronicles series

eBook ISBN-10: 0-9905527-7-2
eBook ISBN-13: 978-0-9905527-7-2
Print ISBN-10: 0-99005527-8-0
Print ISBN-13: 978-0-9905527-8-9

Death by Rum Balls

**Book 4 in
The New Orleans Go Cup Chronicles series**

By Colleen Mooney

Table of Contents

Chapter One

MY NAME IS Brandy Alexander, and I made the mistake of stopping by Julia's to drop off mistletoe, not the fake kind, but the real deal. It was precisely what she'd asked me to buy for her Christmas party tonight. And no, that isn't a stage name, and I don't dance on Bourbon Street. Brandy was my dad's idea of the perfect New Orleans name for a girl with our last name—Alexander. He sat waiting in a bar—and drinking—on the night I was born. His rogue brother, my Uncle Andrew who was with him, thought it was a great name too. My mother, however, did not. She's been blaming me for it my entire life—like I could name myself!

I took a lunch break, which I don't normally do this time of year. Starting on Black Friday, the busiest shopping day of the year, and ending sometime when returns are final after New Years, there is an increase of online shopping, bringing with it more fraudulent activity for companies like mine. My work is in a specialized department for a major telecom organization. My knack for seeing what others miss makes me good in this type of work. I can see calling patterns in dialed numbers. Sometimes the duration of calls is what clues me to investigate further. It involves looking at spreadsheets of dialed numbers for mind-numbing periods of time, but once

I notice an irregularity, I lock onto it like a heat-seeking missile. Online holiday shopping is to hackers what an All You Can Eat Buffet is to those with voracious appetites.

I spotted Frank, Julia's handyman, waving his arms wildly for my attention. It would have been hard not to spot him jumping up and down behind the manger of the life-sized nativity on the front lawn of Julia's bed and breakfast. Squeezing through the shoulder-to-shoulder nutcracker soldiers that lined the walkway I found myself stepping over dozens, if not hundreds, of extension cords that looked like the spaghetti tracks weathermen use for hurricane forecasts.

The fresh, woody fragrance of the spruce tree in the middle of the yard wafted subtly in the cool air. It reminded me of every Christmas since I was born, all spent next door at the Deedlers. Mr. Deedler always brought home a freshly cut spruce tree on Christmas Eve. The smell of spruce always reminded me of Christmas.

Julia's tree which had to be fifty-feet tall if it was an inch had a man working in a cherry picker trying to maneuver a star into position on top of it.

"Brandy!" Frank hissed in his loudest whisper. "Get over here! I have to tell you something."

"Oh, I thought you were waving your arms trying to stay warm out here. Are you trying to hide from Julia because you're not doing a very good job?" I asked as I picked my way across the lawn on my toes, trying to keep my four-inch heels from sinking into the grass.

"Yes, I'm hiding from Julia," he said, and when I got close enough, he grabbed my hand and pulled me behind the manger. In heels, my five-foot-eight height put me right at six feet compared to Frank's five-foot-five elfin frame. While he watched his weight with the tenacity of a runway model, he was strong enough to almost lift me off my feet.

Frank was wearing gloves with the fingers cut off and one of the jumpsuits Julia bought for him to work in. Frank had customized his jumpsuit by bedazzling his name over the pocket in rhinestones. He pulled out a white, linen hanky and sneezed into it. He made a production out of dabbing his nose three or four times on each nostril before folding the square neatly and tucking it back into his bedazzled pocket.

"What are we doing back here, Frank? Cuz I'm not that kinda girl," I said.

"Don't be silly," Frank said while he made this all-a-flutter movement with his hands.

"So, what do you want to tell me that is so important we have to hide behind Hotel Dieu…freezing?" I wanted to hear the *Reader's Digest* version of whatever he had to tell me instead of the epic production Frank could take all afternoon delivering. I was stepping from toe to toe trying to keep my feet from going numb. I scrunched up my shoulders and pulled my coat up over my face to my eyes. Breathing inside my coat was helping me warm up a little. Winter in New Orleans is damp, so it could feel like a bone-crushing cold even if it was only forty degrees.

"I don't want her to come home and see us talking," he sniffed. "She went to lunch with LB, her new boyfriend."

"She's not even home!" My head popped up out of my coat, and I sounded like I was screaming at him because I was. "We're hiding behind a manger. Julia would have to be psychic to know what you're going to say. This really better be important so I have a reason for standing outside instead of being inside…" and raising my voice a tad I added, "where it's warm."

"When I tell you what is happening here, it will curl that straight blonde hair of yours," Frank said. "Nice coat. Looks new, is it cashmere?" he asked rubbing my arm like a cat.

"Yes and yes on the coat. Out with it, Frank. I've got to get back to work, and I'm cold."

"Julia's getting death threats. Maybe it's over all the outdoor decor in the front yard, or maybe it's over the other things that are going on," he said, picking imaginary lint off his jumpsuit.

"Death threats? That's not news. I've threatened to kill Julia many times. Why are other threats newsworthy?" I asked while clapping my gloved hands together in an attempt to keep them warm. Julia had a knack for ticking people off. The comments she made to her manager at the telecom company where we both used to work got her downsized right out the door. I still worked there and we've remained friends, even though it is difficult at times.

"One man from the Neighborhood Business Association told her she was making the neighborhood look like a cheap amusement park. They complained she would force them to hire police for traffic and crowd control to handle all the types of people it would attract." Frank air quoted types. "They said tons of cars coming to see her production will jam up the streets, and they can't get to and from their homes, not to mention it will bring more crime. The neighborhood association sent her this letter telling her to remove it all." He handed it to me to read.

"I guess they're afraid she'll compete with the owner of the local chicken franchise, who turned Christmas lights into neighborhood warfare when he tricked out his home," I said while reading the letter. I flipped the paper over to see if anything was written cryptically on the back. Nada. "You know who they are referring to, right?"

"Yes," Frank said between sniffles and a big eye roll that moved his head around with it.

After reading the demand letter sent by the neighborhood association, I took a minute to look at what they seemed so worked up over. Julia did have a lot of outdoor decorations, more than anyone else, but growing up in New Orleans, people always put out tacky stuff during every holiday.

"We have Mardi Gras for goodness sake," Frank said. "Everyone should be used to tacky by now. What if they make her close the bed and breakfast?" Frank asked more distressed than usual and started pulling at a short piece of hair on the back of his head.

I looked around. There were so many things moving, spinning, blinking, and twinkling that as soon as my eyes moved to the next decoration, I noticed something I missed and had to go back and look at it all again. Even in the daytime the number of lights all over her large mansion turned the bed and breakfast into a thing to behold. I could see every light was equally spaced and faced the same direction. *Who has time to do all this?*

"I don't think it will come to that," I said. "This is Julia's first year of being in her new business, and I think she's excited, that's all." I crossed my fingers behind my back. "There's probably some association rule she's violating and they sent a letter asking her to comply. No big deal."

"No, it's not just the letter. One neighbor complained to her about the traffic." Frank picked up a box resting on the ground near his feet addressed to Julia. "This was left at the front door and there's no return address or sender marked on it. Do you think we should open it?" he asked pushing the package into me. It was thumping like something was hopping around inside.

"Bombs tick, they don't bump around inside a box," I said. "When will she be back?" The way the box was moving gave me the creeps, so I tried to hand it back to him. Frank wouldn't take it so I put it back on the ground. It continued to erratically thump around like something inside wanted out. "It seems something was sleeping and we woke it up."

"She went to lunch with LB about thirty minutes ago and this came right after. What if something is alive in here and dies from no air before she gets back?" he asked.

"Something like what?" I asked. Neither of us could now take our eyes off the box moving around by itself.

"Maybe the boyfriend sent her a puppy? Or a kitten? He knows she's crazy over animals. Maybe it's a Christmas present?" We could not stop looking at the box with its erratic movements. Frank added, "The way things are going, maybe someone wants her to open a box with a dead animal inside."

"Something is alive in there," I said.

"Maybe we should open it and wrap it back up before she comes home. We could put air holes in it." Frank was pulling at that one piece of hair again. "It could be a bird. Julia lost that lovebird she had in her office not long ago. Maybe LB sent her another one."

The box wasn't very heavy, and since I had put it on the ground, it wasn't moving as much. I thought the box was too heavy to be a bird unless it was a fat pigeon. I started to worry if it was a puppy or a kitten, it could suffocate by the time she came home. "Okay, let's open it and put air holes in it. Then we'll wrap it back up so she can be surprised," I said. I nodded toward the box and said to Frank, "You do it."

"Why do I have to do it?" Frank stepped back and put both hands on his chest.

"Cuz you're the boy?" I asked as if it were obvious.

"I'm a girl trapped in a boy's body," he sniffed. "Brandy, you're the fearless one when it comes to handling stuff like this. Please?" Frank took another step away from the box, holding out a pocketknife for me to use.

"Something is just not right about this box," I said. I bent over to work on the box while it remained on the ground. "Frank, get ready to catch a bird if it is one. If what's in here flies away, YOU have to explain it to Julia."

I started to work on the tape with Frank's knife, while he pulled off his fleece jacket and positioned himself to throw it over a bird should one fly out in an attempt to escape. I had barely finished cutting through the tape on one side of the top when the first big, black sewer rat squeezed through the slight opening. I skyrocketed to my feet. Frank and I grabbed onto each other, and we both jumped back at the same time. My heels promptly dug into the lawn. I held onto Frank harder to keep from falling on the ground with the rat. We were frozen in a death grip, hanging onto each other with both hands as we watched two more big, black rodents squeeze out after the first one. We stood staring at the box for what felt like an hour after the third rat vacated and it stopped moving.

I kicked the box to make sure nothing else was inside.

After the rats ran off under the house or into the bushes, our heart rates returned close to normal. I opened the box the rest of the way while Frank took a step backward and watched. 'Rats get what they deserve' was written in the bottom of the box in black marker.

"I wish we hadn't opened it," Frank said.

"I'm sorry we did, too, but can you imagine if she opened that in the house? I bet that is what whoever sent it was banking on," I said. "Who delivered it? Did you see the person?"

"No. After Julia left with LB, I came out because the guys were delivering the tree on the front lawn. I saw it at the front door. It wasn't moving then. When I headed back inside, I came to get it and saw it moving and thumping like you did. I was trying to decide what to do with it right before I saw you drive up. When I saw you stop, I brought the box over here with that letter I just showed you. I didn't want Julia to see me give it to you to read. I was thinking if I let something die in a box while she was gone, she would kill me." Frank made a theatrical gesture of stabbing himself in the chest with an imaginary knife like Julia might do to him. If anything, Julia let Frank get away with murder.

"So, do you know who left this letter?" I asked, looking at Frank through narrowed eyes.

"No. It was left in the mailbox unsealed, you know, with the flap tucked inside. No stamp either," Frank said. Frank was more than a handyman. He was Julia's boy Friday and most of the time he knew more of what was going on at the bed and breakfast than she did.

"Rats?" I was thunderstruck. "Who would send live rats as a Christmas gift?"

"That was no gift. Who would send that to her? Oh, I don't know. Let's see," he said in a mocking tone. He stood tapping a foot, one arm crossed over his body holding his elbow of the other arm in his hand, while one finger rested on his chin. "Maybe one of the neighbors whose kids she called the cops on. Or someone in the cooking club she's browbeating into meeting here to use her oh-so-big-and-perfect kitchen. I heard her telling them that she'd be a terrible cook if she had to work in their kitchens." When he finished, Frank just stood there shaking his head side to side in disapproval.

"Yes, that implies they're all bad cooks and they may not take that too well," I said. "Julia's from Baton Rouge which is not known as the culinary capital of the state. She is gonna get a knife from her perfect kitchen in her back if she isn't careful."

"She told one of her church group ladies…"

"Wait. What?" I cut Frank off. "Julia's in a church group?" Julia had been known to cuss like a drunken sailor when she didn't get her way, so I could not imagine a church group putting up with her for very long or Julia's interest lasting any length of time either. This was bigger news than the rats.

"Hard to imagine, but yes, she is in a church group." Frank looked heavenward when he added, "She wants God in her life since she's trying to meet someone nice, and she thinks that's going to influence Him to send her a rich one." He stopped to cross himself.

"Frank, can we speed this up? It's getting colder out here," I said, blowing hot air into my fists to try to warm them. "My feet feel like blocks of ice," I said and nodded to

Frank's feet which donned low-wedged-heel-pumps with a peek-a-boo toe. "Aren't your feet cold in those?" I asked.

"I'm wearing knee-high hose to keep my feet warm. As I was saying…" Frank stopped with his hands on his hips to make sure I was listening. "One of the church ladies asked what she could bring to the party tonight. She told her to keep her Tupperware home, and she didn't want dips, chips, or pigs in a blanket."

Tack and diplomacy were not on Julia's list of skills. It probably wasn't even on her list of skills she thought she should acquire.

Frank peeked around the manger to see if Julia had come home yet. "I'm worried the neighborhood association might try to close down the bed and breakfast. Then she'll really be difficult to live with," Frank said.

"I'm more worried about the rat thing. That's dangerous and more menacing. One could have bitten her. We could have been bitten," I said moving my pointed finger back and forth between me and Frank. "That's over the top. The Neighborhood Business Association doesn't want to close anybody down and lose tax revenue coming into the area. Besides, church group ladies are more likely to pray for her, so…"

"Not this bunch of do-gooders," Frank cut me off. "They all have rich husbands based on the cars they drive and the clothes they wear. One of them has a Louis Vuitton bag I'd give any…"

"Frank," I cut him off. "I'm cold. Stick to the issues I need to know please."

The moisture from his exaggerated exhales hung between us. "I've overheard them saying Julia is nouveau riche and ill-mannered when she leaves the room. They need their eyes and hearing checked because I'm not invisible *or* deaf." Frank just shook his head making a tsk, tsk, tsk sound. For all his nutty behavior, he was loyal to Julia. He said, "That's not the worst one though."

"There's something worse than rats and hateful church ladies?" I asked.

"Yep. She's been seeing a married man until recently. The Queen," the not so endearing term Frank used for Julia when she was out of audio range, "found out he was married to someone in her gourmet cooking group who is also in her Pilates class. Rather, the wife in Julia's Pilates class found out her husband was seeing Julia when another gourmet club member let it slip—here in this kitchen—during a cooking class. Pilates threw a handful of flour at Julia and then proceeded to throw the entire twenty-pound bag all over the kitchen. Guess who had to clean that up?" Frank paused waiting for me to answer.

"Please, Frank. It's too cold for the pregnant pause," I said.

"I bet she didn't tell you that one, did she?"

"No. She didn't," I said. "Do you think this woman—the wife—is dangerous?"

"I don't know. She was on a tirade that day in our kitchen, and the other cooks ran and grabbed all the knives," he said. "You know how Julia can press the wrong button on people."

"More like she can push all the buttons on the panel," I said.

"Brandy, you see stuff people do all the time. Keep an eye on the others tonight and not just that hot, new boyfriend of yours. Watch Julia's back tonight, please? So will I when she doesn't have me working like a slave."

"I'll be here," I said.

"There's one other thing. She invited her brother."

"The one she doesn't get along with?" I asked as we watched Julia's Mercedes pull into the drive and park all the way in the back of the house.

"Yes. It's the only brother she has." Frank said and continued in a hurry, "The brother and his new wife of two weeks. Julia doesn't know he's married yet. He told me when he called to RSVP to the party."

"Wait. What?" I said just as Julia let her dogs out the front door, all of them. They ran and chased each other through the yard decorations, knocking over everything in their paths.

Frank looked back and forth from the front door to me before he went back to his whisper, "She invited the cooking Pilates and her husband to the party tonight. They're coming."

"Anything else, Frank?" I asked not thinking there could possibly be another issue in Julia's life, but I have been wrong before and I was wrong now.

"Her new boyfriend's name is LB, and there's something just not right about him." Frank said and peeked around the manger again before he said, "Quick. She isn't looking. Go." Then he ran off around the manger in the opposite direction.

My head was spinning from all the people Julia invited to the party, and who, according to Frank, all had a score to settle with her. I was looking forward to having a romantic holiday evening with my new boyfriend, Jiff. Now, Frank wanted me to be Julia's wingman and watch for problems any one of a dozen guests might want to cause at this party tonight.

I allowed myself to be distracted by all the decorations in an attempt to re-clutter my mind with something other than Julia's problems, many of which she didn't even know she had. Every inch of the lawn was decorated. The manger Frank and I hid behind had life-sized people and two sheep that raised and lowered their heads as if eating the bale of hay in front of them. Next to the manger was Santa in a sleigh with eight reindeer as tall as me with several elf characters loading the sleigh with toys. The elves were animated and moved in a circle on some powered track up to the sleigh and appeared to put a toy in it while Santa—who had audio—ho, ho, hoed his approval while his animated arm checked off a list he held in the other hand. There were spotlights on a snowman family surrounded by fake snow to one side of the big tree. They didn't move.

I loved Christmas. I liked all the decorations and enthusiasm Julia had for the holiday. There was nothing like the smell of a real tree. When I was growing up, my mother insisted my dad put up a fake tree in our house and bought all plastic ornaments that were the same color. She had it on a board with rollers she could roll in and out of a closet, throw a sheet over it, and never have to take it down or put it up. If we were still children, my mother would be an early adopter of the huge blow-up lawn monstrosities now popular. The choices were endless. There were blow-up snowmen, or snowmen families, Santas in helicopters, Santas with reindeer, and Santas with toys. Anything you could think of was made to be blown up into Hulk-size plastic proportions—their balloon likenesses tethered to the front lawn by night and deflated by day.

I involuntarily shivered, but it was not from the cold.

Chapter Two

FRANK WENT TO straighten several of Santa's reindeer Julia's dogs had turned over in their enthusiastic romp all over the front yard. I took my time walking to the front door, still taking it all in and watching my step so I didn't twist an ankle in the power cords. Julia opened the front door before I knocked. Her six or seven dogs—I've lost count—ran back to greet me barking, howling, and circling my feet. I hope she hadn't seen Frank and me nose-to-nose behind the manger and start asking questions.

The common denominator for my friendship with Julia was our love for dogs. We rescued them, found homes for them, and helped each other do it. Julia had the patience of Job with dogs. With people, not so much—in fact, not at all. Saying whatever was on her mind is what got Julia fired and caused many of her fellow workers, including her manager, to have an instant dislike of her. I know Julia had it tough growing up and was on her own at an early age. Julia had a big heart as evidenced by taking Frank in and giving him a job, along with the six, or maybe it's seven, stray dogs. She wanted someone in her life as much as I wanted my childhood sweetheart, Dante, in mine. Frank was her handyman of sorts and about the only person who could put up with her on a full-time basis. Too bad for Julia, Frank was gay. Too bad for me, my childhood sweetheart didn't seem to be in any hurry to make our life happen. I was twenty-seven years old and tired of waiting for Dante to decide when and if we should start our life together.

"Come in, come in, it's too cold to be dilly dallying around outside. You can see all that from in here," Julia said in her Baton Rouge accent, which most people confused with Texas. She had big Dallas hair which added to the confusion as to which city she was from.

"Doesn't my tree look beautiful?" she asked.

I thought she meant the tree on the lawn, but she was looking over my shoulder into the double parlor off the entry hall. I turned and saw a smaller version of the ginormous one out front.

"FRANK!" she screamed out the front door while standing next to me.

"You will cause permanent hearing loss if you scream like that again standing so close to me," I said.

Julia ignored me but then yelled one decibel lower, "Frank! Come inside. You need to finish this tree in here. Leave that stuff alone out there."

"That," I said, jerking a thumb toward it like a hitchhiker, "is a really big tree out there. And you have another one in here? Why? Because one skyscraper of a Christmas tree in your yard isn't enough? How big is that thing?"

"The ceilings in here are only fourteen-feet so this tree could only be twelve-feet," Julia answered proudly. "The one outside is maybe fifty-feet but I can't put ornaments outside. No one can see them at night, so I could only have lights and a star. I like to see my ornaments every year, so I put one up inside."

Julia inherited her deceased husband's money—the deceased husband she was in the process of trying to divorce when he kicked the bucket. Lucky for Julia, not so lucky for him. She found a key to a storage unit with suitcases full of cash after he died. She bought a one-hundred-year-old Victorian mansion on Canal Boulevard next to a cemetery and turned it into a bed and breakfast. She renovated it and has been having much success especially after a guest was murdered here, and the media suggested it might be haunted. We were afraid the "haunted" part would kill her business, but with the cemetery next door, it increased tenfold.

"You really have a lot of decorations," I said, looking around as Julia slammed the front door. It reopened as if by magic, and Frank came through it unbothered over the fact that Julia just shut it in his face.

"Hey, Brandy, don't stand still for too long or she'll make me hang an ornament on you," he said. I nodded at Frank as he climbed up the ladder to work on the tree.

"I'm surprised Julia's not making you wear an elf costume to decorate the house."

"You mean a prison elf costume, don't you? I'm in Julia Prison. She makes me wear these jumpsuits. I guess it could be worse; they could be orange," Frank said. He was trying to balance on top of the ladder and untangle the string of lights Julia handed him. "There's more stuff in the boxes than there is space in this house for it." Frank was now fighting with the lights, and the ladder began to precariously wiggle beneath him.

I offered to help pass the lights around the tree to him.

"Don't start helping or she'll drive you into the ground like she does me," he said with an exaggerated slump of his shoulders. "Then you'll be exhausted for tonight." He climbed down and lowered his voice, acting as if Julia wasn't standing right next to me and could not hear what he said, "Get out while you can."

"Don't listen to him. He's not in the holiday spirit," Julia said, smiling and wearing a festive-green, low-cut sweater with black Mirabeau feathers around the scoop neck, a pencil-straight black skirt to below the knee, and black, four-inch high heeled, pumps. She offered to take my coat, and when I handed it to her, she looked my dress up and down and said, "That dress shows off your figure, but something low-cut would be sexier. Red goes well with your blonde hair for the holidays even if it is a work dress."

"Thank you, Julia. I think," I said.

"You could dress it up some with the right jewelry," she said as her gaze took in my shoes and nails when I pulled off my gloves.

"I thought this was the right jewelry," I said. Frank looked at me sideways without moving his head and opened his eyes wide so only I could see him.

"Well, I hope you have something sexier than that to wear tonight," she said, "but not too sexy. I don't want my new man looking at you more than me."

Julia was always in fashion-critique mode. Her world revolved around the right outfit, matching shoes with purse, and the proper accessories, i.e. jewelry—all the time—twenty-four seven. I believed in wearing bling when the occasion called for it. Julia was a "bling on demand" fashionista.

"Brandy will look stunning in anything she wears tonight," Frank said. "And she'll have the best-looking accessory on her arm." He was referring to Jiff and I'm sure that didn't sit well with Julia.

"I'm still on the clock," I said and rubbed my hands together to warm them. The cold was slow to wear off. "I've got to go back to work. You know this is the busiest time of year for me."

"Frank, you're bunching too many lights in one place. Get down and look at them before you have to pull them all off and do it again," Julia said. I thought this was her way of getting even with him for the comment on what I'd be wearing.

Frank had an audio response for everything. He let out another overwhelming sigh as he climbed down the ladder. Even though Julia called Frank a handyman, when she asked him to hang some small pictures in the hall, she had to find larger framed ones to hide the holes he made in the plaster when he missed hammering in the nails. Power tools were out of the question. He was afraid of any tool that required electricity to operate it. Julia was more of a handyman than Frank would ever be.

"What are you doing with your hair for tonight?" Julia asked. "Are you going to have it done this afternoon?"

"I'm going back to work, remember?" I said. "What you see is what you will get tonight, but I'll just be in a nicer dress."

"I hope she wears it down and blown out like she has it now. She has beautiful, shoulder-length blonde hair, Julia. It will look nice however she does it," Frank said in my defense.

He looked at me and nodded toward Julia and said, "She'll be wearing the Dallas hair—like it looks now—only bigger."

Julia ignored Frank.

Frank's skills ran more along the lines of interior decorator and fashion consultant. Julia also made him answer the phone, make or break her appointments, and run errands. It turned out he was also a talented seamstress who could make Julia exquisite outfits without patterns or a machine. He usually wore enough black eye makeup to look like he was a member of a heavy metal band and tonight would be no different. After all, this was a party. He was a thin, small-framed person who wore a different pair of kitten pumps with all his outfits. He had them on now, even if it wasn't the safest footwear for climbing a ten-foot ladder. Good thing Frank was nimble.

When he ran errands for Julia, he took his satchel—Julia and I called it a purse—and wore it New York-style across his chest. Julia would sometimes insist he wear a workman's jumpsuit when she had him doing odd jobs like today. He purchased a Be-Dazzle-R from late night TV and used it to put his name, *Franki*, across the pocket of all his jumpsuits. He would remind us it was Franki with an *I*, no *e*. We both called him Frank. Julia wound up fixing things herself while Frank designed and sewed a new outfit. I desperately needed, and wanted, a Frank in my life.

"Come talk to me in the kitchen while Frank decorates the tree," Julia said.

"Julia, wait. I can't stay. I need to get back to the office and wrap up a few things today. I'll probably even work late. I also need to finish my gift shopping and go to the grocery to get the ingredients for the rum balls I plan to make and bring to Jiff's parents' house for Christmas Eve next week," I said.

"Oh, Miss la tee da," she teased. "You're going to his parents' house? The ones who live on hoity-toity Audubon Place…*with* their own security guard twenty-four seven on their private street?" she asked with added emphasis.

"Yes. That is where they live," I said. Julia put way too much emphasis on appearances and noted who had what and more of it. My stomach had knots in it from just the mention that I was going there to spend our first holiday together. A sense of dread crept up and squeezed my heart knowing I was not going to be with Dante and his family.

"How are you going to get past the guard shack if you don't go with Jiff?" she asked. "Do they have a fingerprint or eyeball scan you have to do to be let in? How did Dante take that news?"

I ignored her until I heard Dante's name and came screeching back to the present as Julia barreled on, "Isn't this the first time y'all won't be spending your annual ten-minute allotment together on Christmas Eve before he gets called off to a homicide?" she asked. "This will be quite a change for you, won't it, spending all of Christmas Eve together with someone?"

She was right. Dante and I spent time together in between his homicide calls, and in New Orleans those were frequent. I was tired of him leaving me as soon as he got a call about a murder. It was a dead body for goodness sake. It wasn't going anywhere. I was the live body he should have been paying attention to.

"Tell Dante we all said Merry Christmas when you do see him," Frank said, trying to squash Julia's insensitivity. "I know you'll see him sometime over the holidays."

Her comments launched memories of every Christmas since I was born spent with Dante's family. We grew up next door to each other and our families still live side by side. Mrs. Ruth, his mom, made pralines and fudge and let us eat all we wanted. His dad brought home a real tree, and all the boys helped him set it up and put the colored lights on it. Dante and I helped put the glass ornaments on the tree Mrs. Ruth had collected from her family and for each of her children. She had baby stockings for each of her sons with their names embroidered on them. She even had a stocking for me from the first Christmas I was brought home from the hospital. Mrs. Ruth had all boys and she adored me since she always wanted a girl. Both our families expected Dante and me to set the date every year and so did I.

Julia rambled on, not waiting for a response from me. This was vintage Julia. "All the homes on Audubon Place are bigger than this place, and I have eight bedrooms. You better go buy some fancy desserts at a French bakery and put it on a nice holiday plate you plan to leave there. Get a nice platter from Macy's or the Hallmark gift store. Don't buy something cheap and plastic or you will look like you're going to a covered-dish dinner," she said, pointing at the tree where she wanted Frank to put more lights. Julia had a knack for making everything special you thought about doing feel ordinary.

"Julia, give me some credit. Here's the mistletoe—real mistletoe, not the fake stuff—you asked me to pick up if I saw any," I said, feeling like I wanted to throw it at her. Frank gave me a big doe-eyed look of sympathy from his perch on top of a ten-foot ladder.

"Thanks," Julia said, taking the mistletoe and inspecting it closely to see if it met her "real vs. fake" approval. After she sniffed it to ascertain its authenticity, she continued, "Didn't they have any that looked a bit fresher than this?"

Frank dropped the string of lights he was wrestling with, and the sound of breaking glass got her attention, along with an icy stare from me. I'm sure Frank was making the universally known move of the finger across his throat for her to cut it out behind me.

"Oh, this is fine. At least it's real. I know exactly where I'm going to hang it. I think I'll put it in the doorway to this room. That way everyone who comes to look at the tree will pass under it," she said looking up at the doorframe we were standing closest to.

"If you hang it now, I'm not going to kiss you or Frank if I walk under it," I said in an attempt to lighten my mood, but it went totally ignored by both of them.

"Brandy, I've got to work on my crown roast for tonight. You ever fix a crown roast? None of those in my gourmet cooking class knew what a crown roast was," Julia said as she handed the mistletoe to Frank and pointed to where she wanted it hung. Then she left for the kitchen without waiting for an answer to any of her questions or thanking me for buying it for her.

"CROWN ROAST, CROWN roast, crown roast. I'm sick of hearing it. She's all impressed with herself for having a crown roast," Frank almost shouted it. Then he lowered his voice and crooked his finger for me to come closer. I don't know why since he didn't care if she heard his opinion of the crown roast.

Frank said in his lowered voice, "I'm worried about this party. I'm worried something terrible is going to happen."

"I'll be here to run interference with Julia and her thoughtless comments. You know, if she keeps bringing up Dante, I might be the one who does something terrible to her," I said and we both smiled at our shared secrets.

"Don't mention any of what I told you outside. See if she tells you about the affair, the neighborhood association, or her brother and the inheritance. She invited all of them to the party."

"What inheritance? From her dead husband? I know about that," I said.

"No, her dad. He died not long ago. She just found out about the inheritance a couple of days ago, and when her brother gets here, she'll find out about his wife. I'm surprised she didn't tell you about her dad," Frank said.

"I am, too," I said. "Don't worry, Frank. Pilates with the philandering husband won't come…"

"They're coming," Frank said.

"Why in the world would she invite all of these people to her party? The bigger question is why would they come?"

"She invited them because she doesn't realize how insulting she is and how much they dislike her for it," Frank said just above a whisper. "Yes, all the people I told you about have RSVP'd and said they are coming. They'll come because they're hoping something bad or embarrassing happens to her and they want to be here to see it. I have a bad feeling one of these people might be behind making something bad happen. I'm glad you and that hot boyfriend of yours will be here so she'll have at least two more people watching her back besides me.

Chapter Three

M Y CELL PHONE started ringing just as I got in my car to rush through an errand before I went back to work. It was Dante's private number, not the precinct's main number he called me from that usually said, NO CALLER ID. I let it go to voice mail. Dante was very intuitive when it came to murderers but had no understanding how lapses of days or weeks, let alone a month, with no communication had negative effects on women, in particular on me, the one he was supposed to be dating.

I still got knots in my stomach when I saw Dante or heard his name and thought of what could have been. I was working very hard at moving on. Dante, on the other hand, acted like nothing had changed.

My phone pinged and a text read *Call me asap. I have five minutes before I have to get back into a meeting.* Great, another snippet of my time with Dante sandwiched in between dead bodies.

As a New Orleans homicide detective, Dante was good at his job and rose quickly through the ranks. He was recently promoted to captain and I hadn't heard from him in weeks after his promotion. The department was always short-staffed and business was booming. New Orleans has always had a healthy crime rate, but now we were seeing crime scenes with multiple shootings and fatalities all over the news.

He picked up on the first ring. "Brandy. Hey, I know I haven't had time to call you for a few days…" he was saying when I cut him off.

"Dante, it has been weeks since we last spoke. I haven't heard from you since… since, well…it was after Halloween and before Thanksgiving," I said, trying not to let the edge from the electric carving knife my dad uses to slice the holiday turkey slip into my voice.

"I've been busy with this new job and all the additional responsibilities," he said. When I didn't answer or comment he asked, "How was your Thanksgiving?"

"I spent it with Jiff and his family," I said. Jiff Heinkel was the guy I had kissed at a parade last Mardi Gras. Dante was working the detail that night along the parade route standing right in front of us when I kissed Jiff. I started dating Jiff because I realized my life with Dante was going nowhere…fast.

"Yeah. Um, I wanted to talk to you about Christmas. I wanted you to know that I'm in Houston all week for a meeting on a joint task force. It's all the captains from both states and we're trying to…"

I could hear a loudspeaker asking attendees to return to their seats. Great, his partner Hanky had told me to hang in there because once Dante was promoted, he would have more time for us to spend together, have holidays, get married, start a family, blah, blah, blah.

"Look, they are about to start the meeting up again and I gotta get back. I might not be back home in time for Christmas Eve this year," he said. The loudspeaker broke in again and was more urgent in the announcement this time. He said, "I really have to go, but I'll try to call you later," and he hung up.

A heavy feeling of dread filled my chest with pain and squeezed my heart until I could barely breathe when I realized I was still hanging onto Dante's every unspoken word.

Chapter Four

I ASKED JIFF to take me to Julia's party. We've been dating since Mardi Gras and exclusively since Thanksgiving. He made no secret of where he wanted our relationship to go. He's a New Orleans gentleman and insists that I wait for him to open my car door when he drives me anywhere.

We arrived at Julia's house for the party and I sat waiting and waiting for the car door to be opened. When I looked over my shoulder to see what might have happened, I saw Jiff standing frozen behind the car facing Julia's mansion looking at the Christmas decorations all over her front lawn. Even though I had been by earlier and had seen the extravaganza, I had not seen it in all of its illuminated wonder. I opened my own door and got out of the car. He was wide-eyed in disbelief at all the moving, twinkling, spinning stuff, along with the holiday music playing loudly over the outdoor speakers. His long, black cashmere coat, scarf, and leather gloves had him rather toasty while he spectated.

I noticed he was staring at the giant spruce in the middle of the front lawn—all fifty, fabulous feet of it.

"I think we better call Rockefeller Center and tell them where they can find their tree," he finally said when I stood next to him. He was still staring at the tree.

"Does all this remind you of anything?" I asked.

"Oh, I'm sorry. I left you in the car," he said. I waved him off as no big deal. "Yes, it does remind me of something. It's reminiscent of the guy who owned the Chicken Kings all over town. His house is what my sister and brothers wanted our house to look like," he said. "The media called him King of Fried Chicken… and the King of Christmas Lights."

"Yes, and King of Neighborhood Discord. Remember when he had Entergy run additional power to his house so he could add more lights and project movies on the side of his house? You could see the glow radiating from as far away as LaPlace. He had to hire details of cops to direct traffic through his neighborhood," I said.

"The City of New Orleans loved him while his neighbors hated him," Jiff said.

"I think that's what Julia's neighborhood association is afraid of. They sent her a letter."

"Well, it's probably a demand letter and they should give her thirty to sixty days to comply. By then, Christmas will be over and she will have taken all this stuff down. If she has any problems, tell her to call me. I'll get an extension for her," Jiff said. He stood still marveling at the front yard not mindful of my teeth chattering from the cold. "How long did it take her to get this done? It must have taken an an army with ladders to put that many Christmas lights in the bushes, all over the house, and the roof. This house is a monstrosity." He leaned into a bush to get a better look at the lights around a window. "Look at this. They must have been out here with a tape measure. The lights are all equally spaced and facing the street."

"I'm freezing out here," I finally said.

"Sorry, it's just so, so…"

"Over the top, like everything she does," I said cutting him off. "You have represented Julia in the past," I said, referring to the recent murder charge she was wrongfully arrested for, "and you still make an offer to help her with the demand letter? Don't you remember how difficult she is?"

Jiff is a criminal attorney with his dad's firm, and he did me a favor representing Julia. Jiff was holding my arm with one hand as we made our way to the front door. We moved slowly, distracted by something with each step along the way.

"Are you sure we've seen it all?" he asked. "Let's stop a minute so we can make sure. I don't want to miss anything, and I will personally warm you up when we get inside." I loved Christmas lights and outdoor decorations, and it was wonderful to have someone who wanted to take extra time to enjoy them with me. My dad would put lights up every year on our house and I would help him. It got both of us outside of the house and away from my mother's wacky behavior. While Jiff stood taking it all in, I tried to count the number of objects all over the front yard.

Jiff looked around the entire front of the house and said, "This must be an obstacle course for her dogs to maneuver around when she lets them out. I don't guess she has a back yard."

"You're right, so she's not hiding any more decorations back there." I looked around and said, "At my house, I threw three strings of white lights in the garden and hung another around the front door. I feel so inadequate now." More to myself than to Jiff I added, "I think my house looks pretty. When the wind blows, even a little, the light twinkles in the monkey grass."

"I like your house," he said and kissed my hand. "It has you in it."

He always knew the exact right thing to say and he was there to say it. When he kissed my hand, it warmed me from the tips of my frozen toes all the way to my nose, rosy from the icy air.

Julia was an equal opportunity holiday decorator. Every holiday tradition known to man in this season was represented.

"I thought she was having a small party," Jiff said.

"Julia never does anything small. She said she was having a few people over to meet her new boyfriend," I said pointing out the nativity I hid behind earlier with Frank. "That manger is the size of the shed I park my car in."

"She had a man with a cherry picker topping the tree with a giant star when I came by earlier," I said. "He started on the tree as I was leaving."

"Of course she did," Jiff said smiling and pulled me close to him.

"Do you think it will freeze tonight?" I asked him. The night was not freezing by the National Weather Service standards, but by New Orleanian standards, anything that dipped below fifty degrees was cause for alarm. It was in the low forties which made everyone worry if we should trickle the water in case freezing temperatures pounced upon us. This was cold for New Orleans, and Jiff and I both had on an overcoat, a scarf, and gloves.

"No, I don't think it will," he said pulling me closer. "Did you hear the news or weather saying it might?"

"No, but I had Frank come over and wrap the exposed pipes under the house I rent with Suzanne a couple of weeks ago, so I'm not worried about a freeze or a pipe bursting.

We'll be home early enough for me to run a trickle of water anyway," I said. As soon as the mercury got anywhere near forty degrees, all of New Orleans worried about their pipes freezing. Raised houses, like the shotgun double I lived in on one side, were especially vulnerable but easier to repair than pipes freezing under a slab.

"I have a better idea of what to do to warm you up. Remind me to show you when I bring you home," he said and squeezed my hand.

Under the gigantic Christmas tree appeared to be a village scene that looked like Santa's workshop in the North Pole. There were lighted dolls, bikes, toy trucks, brightly papered presents, and a train big enough for a small child to ride on going around the tree on a track.

Jiff nodded for me to look up at a Star of David among the dozen or so illuminated falling stars hanging in the large, sprawling oak limbs. "She's covered all the bases," he said and started to move me again to the front door. The walkway was covered in at least one hundred extension cords to power everything from Santa to dozens of spotlights on the mansion—enough to circle the globe twice.

"This is a lawsuit waiting to happen," he said.

"Julia makes a lot of her own problems," I said, thinking of the conversation Frank and I had earlier.

He stopped and pulled me into him and gave me a kiss that took the chill of the night right off of me. Every time he kissed me it had that same effect, just like our first kiss. When our eyes met that first time during a Mardi Gras parade, he stopped dead in his tracks. He looked at me until I walked right up to him and kissed him without knowing his name. That is not uncommon during parades because the men often exchange a kiss for a flower. What was unusual was him whispering in my ear asking me to meet him at the end of the parade, and I did.

He said, "I'm looking forward to this party and having a great time with you."

At the front door, two life-sized nutcrackers stood on either side of the entrance. The leaded glass doors had been festooned in holiday wreaths, lighted garland, and bells. "I don't remember these here earlier when I stopped by," I said. "These guys are taller than Frank. I wonder how he wrestled them out here?"

Before we knocked, I turned to look again just to make sure I didn't miss anything. Even the mailbox had been decorated in lights with a puddle of fake snow resting on the top with "PUT LETTERS TO SANTA HERE" in peel-and-stick lettering on each side, while the pole itself was wrapped to make it look like a candy cane.

"Look at the mailbox. Something is sticking out of it," I said.

"I'll go see. Wait here. We want to make sure Santa gets all the letters." He came back with a rectangular-shaped, gold foiled gift box wrapped only in a gold-wired ribbon. The card on it read:

From your Secret Santa: I hope this gets you what you deserve for the holidays.

"That's an odd greeting on a gift," Jiff said.

"Let me see that," I said and took the box away from Jiff. I pulled the gold ribbon off and handed it back to him.

"Open this." When I saw the way he was looking at me I added, "Please."

"Brandy, are you all right?" he asked me with his eyebrows drawn together.

"I'm good. Please. Just open the box," I said.

Jiff lifted the lid on the gold foil box, while watching me while I watched the box. When he drew back the top, there was gold tissue paper hiding what was inside.

"Just move that paper," I said.

"I don't think we should be opening someone else's…"

I cut him off. "Lift that paper, move the paper. Just do it." I held my breath.

He lifted the paper to reveal a plastic airtight bag of a dozen or so rum balls.

"Good, that's good." I said as I grabbed Jiff's hand holding the gold tissue paper and put it back in the box. I took the top he had handed me and fumbled putting the snug-fitting lid back in place.

Jiff took the box out of my hands and replaced the lid. Then he held it for me to replace the ribbon. He didn't say a word as I pulled my gloves off to complete tying the bow. My hands shook.

"Okay. That's good. You think that looks good?" I asked him in rapid fire.

"Yeah. You wanna tell me what this is about?" Jiff took the box and held my arm.

"I will, later. Let's enjoy this party." I shivered as a chill traveled up my legs, stopping at my shoulders and said, "We need to give that to Frank."

Chapter Five

W E RANG THE bell, arriving fashionably late by thirty minutes. I told Jiff about the neighborhood association letter, but I had not mentioned any of the other crazy stuff Frank told me earlier. I didn't really want to tell him about the rats because, truthfully, I wanted to forget it. If he knew I thought there was something other than a gift in the gold foil box (like a dead rat), he would have tossed it in the trash. This was our first Christmas together since we met, and I wanted to enjoy this party with him. I didn't want any of Julia's self inflicted foolishness to spoil it. It appeared I would be spending the entire holiday with him and that suited him just fine. I had not mentioned to my family that Dante and I would not be joined at the hip and visit both families this Christmas Eve—the first Christmas Eve ever.

Julia and her nutty problems would have to wait until after this evening *if* she even wanted my help with any of it.

There was already a crowd of people inside visible through the floor-to-ceiling windows across the front porch. The double leaded glass entry doors swung open, and a man in a ten-gallon hat wearing a western bolo necktie stood there. He was easily six feet, five inches tall under the hat. He grabbed Jiff by the hand, shaking it so vigorously that Jiff's head looked like a bobble-head doll for a second. He turned his attention to me and wrapped two big, flabby arms around me saying, "You've gotta be Brandy. Gimme a kiss you little filly. Any friend of Julie's is a friend of mine. You can call me LB."

Julie? He called her Julie, not Julia. I wondered how that was going to play with her. And, he was wearing a hat—a rather large, hard-to-miss hat—inside. He was not wearing his manners.

It was a good thing Julia had a house with fourteen-foot ceilings so the hat could clear the doorways. He took off before asking to take our coats or scarves. I hung our things on one of the coat hooks in the center hallway. We spotted LB in one of the large double parlors as he made his way to find Julia. It was hard to miss the hat.

The other guests were all dressed casually-elegant as the invitation suggested for the party. Ladies had on slacks with beaded tops or holiday sweaters. The men had on sport coats without ties. Some had on shirts with ties and no coats. I recognized the couple that lived across the street from Julia. Janice had a scowl on her face while Ned was holding a glass of red wine that matched the healthy glow on his smiling face. I smiled and waved a hello as we passed them following ten-gallon hat on his mission to find Julia.

Julia was glamorous in a gold beaded dress that sparkled in the party lighting, dimmed for effect. It was fitted and showed off her figure which had been augmented in areas where nature had not been generous. The front had a scoop neck with a very low back, cut almost to the waist. Frank did an amazing job on this one. Even at five eleven in stocking feet, add the four-inch heels she was wearing and the big hair (another four inches) and ten-gallon hat was still taller than she was. Of course, he had to keep the hat on for that to work.

She had on all her bling, meaning tons of jewelry she had gotten as gifts from men she had dated when they broke it off with her. The baubles were sort of parting gifts when her suitor wanted to end the relationship. The idea was to make Julia feel it was her idea to break it off with them, because if she felt she was the one being dumped, then she went "all Julia" on them. "All Julia" was just another term for stalking or exacting revenge by way of calling his new girlfriend or new wife and telling her what gifts he had given her…recently. I'd seen it happen once and it wasn't pretty.

After we cheek to cheek kissed, Julia said, "Look at my Christmas present." She lifted her hand to wave a multi-strand tennis bracelet under my nose with several rows of diamonds. "I see you met my fella. LB this is Brandy and Jiff."

The twang in LB's accent and the ten-gallon hat said he was from Texas to me.

I made all the required "oohs" and "ahs" to indicate how beautiful I thought the bracelet was.

"What an unusual combination of diamonds. Five rows and they alternate between marquis and pear-shaped," I said admiring the piece. "It's stunning."

Jiff said to LB, "You have great taste in jewelry and women." I could have sworn LB's big, loud laugh made the crystal chandeliers tinkle.

The bracelet had to set LB back thousands. What kind of man buys a gift like that for a woman he just met? Something seemed off. Neither one looked that head over heels about each other.

"Your suit is beautiful," Julia said to me while Jiff was laughing it up with LB. "With that neckline you will make all the boys smile. Very festive."

The slightly off-the-shoulder v-neckline revealed a little more cleavage than I felt 100 percent comfortable exposing. After all, I'm a product of the New Orleans Catholic School system, but I wasn't a nun. I felt devilishly sexy in it.

It was a red two-piece silk suit with beading all over the top and sleeves. Jiff bought it for me on one of our Christmas shopping trips downtown to Canal Place a week ago. His offices are in the building complex on one of the top floors, and he asked me to meet him for dinner.

We went shopping before dinner, and he asked me to help him find a new tie for him to wear during the holidays. He pointed out the suit in the window at Saks and persuaded me to try it on. When I got to the ladies' couture department, it was already waiting for me in a dressing room to try on. The dresser who helped me in the fitting room deftly kept the price tag out of my line of vision. When I twirled around modeling it for Jiff, he said, "It's perfect for the holidays." I was about to tell him it was probably out of my budget during the holidays or anytime of the year when he said, "You have to have something red to wear during the season. I knew you'd look amazing in it so it's my treat. Merry Christmas a little early. You can wear it to any or all the parties we go to, but please, I'd like for you to wear it to my parents' house on Christmas Eve."

"I guess this means we're spending Christmas together?" I had asked.

"I'm asking you to spend Christmas Eve with me only if you will wear this to my parents' home. Will you?"

"Yes." I said feeling guilty that I made plans not to be with Dante this Christmas Eve, even though I didn't know at the time he would be out of town and not be able to make plans with me.

How could I refuse when I felt like a million dollars in this suit or refuse a man who showered me with more attention in one day than I ever had in my entire life. I always felt like I didn't deserve the attention, the gifts, someone caring this much for me. It wasn't what I grew up with or how Dante ever made me feel.

Jiff wore a bespoke suit made of a medium-weight black wool and the beautiful red silk tie I'd chosen that matched the color of my suit. His shirts were custom fitted with his initials on the sleeves. He was good-looking, tall, and fit. Most people thought so, not just me. Other women flirted and fell over him, but he was always a polite, consummate gentleman. I knew he adored me and I liked it.

"None of your neighbors get into the spirit like you do. You need to encourage them to get with the program," Jiff said to Julia.

Uh oh. Maybe I should have briefed him on the entire neighborhood's lack of enthusiasm over Julia's winter wonderland display and not just the business association letter.

Frank appeared wearing black, wide-flaring, palazzo pants, a white tux shirt, a rhinestone bowtie, and eyeliner a la the lead singer in KISS. He had on silver kitten pumps. He was carrying a large, rectangular-shaped silver tray with handles on which were about a dozen champagne-filled flutes.

"That's because the neighborhood association has a rule against putting up any outside decorations that aren't voted on and approved," Frank said, jumping into the conversation. "They all voted to put luminaries throughout the neighborhood, all along the streets in the entire neighborhood, even up and down the driveways. They even pay for them and have volunteers to do it. The flier says it's to create a stately elegant holiday neighborhood atmosphere."

"Not everyone voted on the luminaries," Julia snapped and took a glass of champagne. "I'm not listening to the Decoration Nazis." She saw another guest across the room waving her over, and excused herself. Jiff was about to hand her the gold foil gift he took out of the mailbox, and I put my hand on his arm to stop him. He looked at me when I stopped him and I smiled.

"Would you put that in the kitchen for me when you get a chance?" Frank asked, raising his overly arched eyebrows and lifting his hands that held the tray of champagne flutes a few inches to make the point. "I hope it's not like the other surprises she's been getting today."

"What other surprises?" Jiff asked, looking from Frank to me.

I shrugged my shoulders and shook my head in an attempt to feint ignorance, but Frank couldn't wait to tell Jiff. "Julia got another handwritten note this afternoon demanding that she take down her blasphemous and cheap decorations." Frank air quoted blasphemous and cheap with one hand, holding his serving tray with the other. "It was signed, 'A Christian Neighbor.'"

I hoped to God Frank wouldn't mention the rats.

"Blasphemous? How are Christmas decorations blasphemous?" Jiff asked. "They are a tad bit over the top, and a little tacky, but don't these people live here and haven't they seen Mardi Gras?"

"I know, right?" Frank said in agreement. "That's because last night someone arranged two of the reindeer together to look like rutting season in the front yard." He added, "And, no, it wasn't me" when Jiff and I both dropped our jaws and looked up over our champagne glasses at him.

"It was probably one of the neighborhood kids playing a prank," Frank went on. "They do stuff to annoy her on a weekly basis. They've rolled this place in toilet paper twice."

Frank had the skinny on everything, so I asked, "Did any of the neighbors she had issues with RSVP and say they were coming to the party?"

"Only the ones who speak to her," Frank said. "It's a very short list."

"I see the neighbors from across the street are here. Janice doesn't seem like she's in a festive mood," I said.

"That's because Julia flirts with Ned to get him to help her move furniture around. Then she can't be bothered if Janice asks to borrow something. Julia tells her she doesn't have it," Frank said. "I once heard her tell Janice, 'Why don't you just order out? Ned says you're not much of a cook.'"

"Why am I friends with her?" I thought I had said that to myself, but Frank and Jiff looked at me. "You heard that?" They nodded yes. "Pinky swear you won't tell her," and we all locked our little fingers.

Frank answered, "You're friends because of the dogs. Brandy, you're too nice and you put up with her because she likes dogs, and you think she can't be all that bad because she loves animals. I'm here to tell you—she can." Frank's eyes scoped out the room and when he saw Julia he said, "The

Queen is giving me the evil eye so I need to get back to being the Waiter Elf." A couple came over and he offered them champagne. They each took a flute, smiled at us, and walked off. "Wait till you get a look at the brother and his new wife," Frank said.

"Which one is he?" I asked.

"You'll know him instantly. He's the one in the flop sweat," Frank said over his shoulder as he went back to serve the other guests.

"Julia has a brother?" Jiff asked.

"Yep. One that's apparently in a flop sweat," I said. "Whatever that is."

"I thought Julia was the black sheep of her family," he said in a way causing his eyes to twinkle.

"Oh no," I said. "Not compared to him." I took a step back to get even further away from the people standing in the room near us. "I don't want this to be overheard. I've never met him. This is all based on what Julia has told me. Her brother, Larry, works in the oil field selling some kind of equipment they use on the rigs. She says he makes a lot of money," I said. "These are Julia's words, not mine. She says he's a beer drinker who frequents honky tonks and chases women. His type… topless dancers or wives of other men." Remembering what Frank enlightened me with earlier, I thought Julia might have more in common with her brother than she cared to admit based on her recent illicit affair.

"Ok, he must be a rough customer," Jiff said.

"Again, Julia's words are Little Larry, he was named after his dad, Larry, also got his dad's temper and personality. They both work things out using their fists. Julia left home when she was fifteen which explains why she has poor skills relating to people. She's been on her own ever since."

"Why did she invite him?" Jiff asked.

"All I can say is," I took a deep breath because some of my past holiday memories were both nostalgic and painful, "and this is speaking from experience, the holidays make women do weird stuff. It puts our hormones in overdrive, pulling at our nesting genes or maternal genes, whatever it is that makes us want to cook, bake, buy the perfect gifts, decorate the entire house in a ton of stuff like this, and visit people we would normally avoid the rest of the year."

"So, do you have plans with your family? And, am I invited?" he asked.

"I don't have any plans at the moment, but if I do anything more than drop off their gifts, I will let you know. You've met my family. Why do you want to do that again?" I asked.

"Well, I'll leave that up to you," he said.

"My mother and sister have never liked anything I've given them no matter the effort or expense I have gone to in order to give them something nice. Every year they ask where can they return it as soon as it is unwrapped. This year I'm dropping off gift certificates," I said.

"Well, I hope whatever stuff the holiday makes you want to do, it makes you want to do it with me," Jiff said and squeezed my hand. "This Christmas is already perfect for me now that you are in it."

I leaned into his ear and whispered, "Oh yes, I'm all warm and gooey inside right now." I squeezed his hand in return and said, "Come on, let's go mingle."

We moved around trying to meet some of the other guests and introduce ourselves to people. We met Bicky who said she was in Julia's Pilates class and the cooking class.

"For all the good the cooking class does, most of us just drink wine while Julia tells us how we've been doing it all wrong," Bicky said. "My husband and kids are still alive, so I guess I might be doing something right."

"I just cook what I like to eat," I said. "He takes us out to restaurants, mostly," I nodded toward Jiff and introduced them.

Bicky's husband said his name was Matt, and other than one or two exchanges about the Saints and LSU with Jiff, he wasn't very talkative. Bicky sipped her wine and smiled.

A couple came in after us, left their coats in the hallway, and came directly over to where we four were standing. Bicky introduced the couple as Matt's sister, Sheila, and her husband Patrick MacFinn. She also made a point of telling Shelia that I was a good friend of Julia's.

Shelia MacFinn was a beautiful, statuesque woman and dressed like she was about to walk down a runway. Where Bicky had an edge about her, Sheila was glamorous. She was warm and friendly, especially so after she found out I was Julia's friend. Patrick was nice looking, thirty-something, and dressed the part of investment banker, attorney, or whatever uptown family business he was embroiled in.

After a few minutes of small talk, and I left that mostly to Jiff, we politely moved along in search of refills for our wine.

Most of the guests who showed up were cordial but not too friendly. I wondered why they even bothered to come to a party. Since I knew Ned and Janice, I took Jiff over to introduce him to them.

"I thought you dated a cop," Ned said and grabbed a handful of nuts off a nearby table. He tossed them into his mouth.

"Ned!" Janice jumped in and the scowl turned into a weak smile. Janice and Ned adopted a rescued schnauzer from me. Julia had suggested it back when she found out they lost their poodle of fifteen years.

"You mean my friend Dante. You have a good memory. Dante came with me when I brought you that little rescued schnauzer I named Kringle. That was right after Julia bought this place," I said. I started thinking about Kringles from the bakery I named Janice and Ned's schnauzer after. The Kringle is similar to the King Cake we have at Mardi Gras. They are oval shaped with a cinnamon dough base much like a King Cake, but instead of purple, green, and gold sugar sprinkled on top, they are covered in brown maple sugar and pecans. They are more decadent than their Mardi Gras cousin. The thought made me feel the need for a giant sugar fix. I'm sure Julia had one on the dessert buffet. I wanted to go search for it, but I tuned back in when I heard the mention of another adoption.

"We spoil her rotten, and we kept that name since we got her during the holidays," Ned said, and now Janice was smiling and nodding in agreement. "We even talk about getting her a playmate."

"Well, that's great. Why don't you come to the Holiday Yappy Hour tomorrow evening at the feed and seed store on Jefferson Highway? It's a fundraiser for rescues. It's a ten-dollar donation and they serve wine and cheese. They have dog treats for our pets. There will be a Santa Paws and photos," I said.

"Brandy and I are going so we can take a holiday photo together with our dogs. She's bringing Meaux and I have a schnauzer named Isabella," Jiff said. "Rescue is the reason I first saw Brandy and found out who she was. I saw her bring a rescued schnauzer to a man in my building, and I asked him all about her. I thought she was pretty and doing a good thing. I was trying to figure out how to meet her when a strange set of circumstances brought us together," he said while looking at me, and then he brought up my hand he was holding and kissed it.

"I guess a strange set of circumstances brought us together too," Janice said looking in the direction of Julia. "Ned, come with me to get another drink, not that you need one," She walked off as Julia and her cowboy-hat-wearing boyfriend moved in our direction.

Before I could ask ten-gallon hat what brought him to New Orleans, I heard, "Does everyone in Colorado wear a hat like that, even inside?"

We all turned to see who had asked the question, and I thought it had to be Julia's brother, Larry. I had never met him, but he had Julia's eyes and looked every bit as she described him. He was a tall, husky guy, and a little past the point of being fit. In other words, he had the start of a healthy beer investment about to bulge over his blue jeans. He wasn't as heavy a man as LB, but close. He also wore a flannel shirt and cowboy boots. He combed his hair with some sort of gel or paste that made it look like it was still wet from the shower. I could smell it from where I was standing. It had a clinical sort of odor, not anything like a man's cologne, more like a scalp treatment, and he was perspiring, a lot. So much so it showed in his armpits in the shape of large, wet half moons and down the front of his shirt in a V. He pulled a handkerchief from his back pocket and wiped the sweat running down his forehead before he extended his hand to shake with LB.

Ten-gallon hat stuck out his big, fleshy hand to shake Larry's and said, "I'm guessing you must be my Julie's little brother."

Chapter Six

"YEP. YOU ARE a good guesser," Larry said. "But you better call her Julia; that's her name, not Julie. She might take your head off, hat and all."

"No, he's not a good guesser," Julia replied, looking at her brother and ignoring the other comment about her name. "I told him you would be the only one to come to a fancy Christmas party in jeans and boots. Larry, why don't you go change your shirt?"

Larry ignored Julia's suggestion but turned to her and asked, "What cha put in these here rum balls, Sis? They really warm ya' up." By way of introduction, he wrapped one arm around the shoulders of the woman standing next to him. "This here is Donna, my new wife. Her stage name is Twilight. We been married just two weeks." The woman had black, Goth hair teased within an inch of its frizzy life and was wearing an outfit straight out of a Frederick's of Hollywood's Christmas catalog. It was a skin-tight, red spandex bodysuit with a big heart-shape cutout at the neckline that her cleavage was trying to escape through. The heart was outlined in rhinestones. There were white fake fur cuffs on the sleeves at the wrists. She looked like someone Santa might fantasize about in his dreams during the off season. Who am I kidding? Santa or any man would fantasize about her in any season. She was sporting a black eye that all the stage makeup in the world could not hide. She also had a healthy glow about her, as my Dad would say about women who perspire.

Julia turned to Twilight and finally said, tapping her own eye, "Boy, I bet that was hard to cover up in your wedding photos."

"I just took profile photos," Donna Twilight said.

"Larry, you got yourself a fast thinker here," said Julia. The mocking went right over both their heads. Julia waved Frank over and told him to go let the dogs out of the back room now that everyone had arrived.

Frank said, "Maybe you should keep them back there. Some people are afraid of dogs and yours are all big."

"Everybody here knows I love dogs," Julia snapped. "If they don't like my dogs, they can leave." I thought Julia might be hoping Twilight was afraid of dogs and would ask Larry to go home. It didn't happen.

Julia was just standing there looking at them, and I could see her brother start to fidget and look uncomfortable since neither one of them had any idea how to make or fake small talk. Twilight just stood there holding a box of rum balls.

"Looks like we have som-pin in common," Donna Twilight said to Julia. "I love dogs too," she said. Only when she said dogs it sounded more like dawgs. While Julia did love dogs, I didn't think Donna's revelation of having this in common with her new sister-in-law endeared Donna Twilight to Julia in any way.

Julia had six dogs at last count, but did she keep the one she picked up off the interstate? I couldn't remember. They were all big except one medium-sized yappy dog. Six dogs, or seven, were too many by popular opinion. Most were hounds so they howled instead of barked. I heard them howling from the back of the house when we arrived. When she let them run through the house, it felt like a pack of thirty wild hyenas yapping and barreling past you instead of six or seven.

"How did you two meet?" Ten-gallon hat jumped in and asked them. Since we were standing together for the first time all evening, I noticed how much older he looked than Julia. Age and time had not been kind to his face which appeared to have been reworked by years of hard experiences. He seemed like he was making an effort to be agreeable with Julia's rogue brother.

"I met my bride speed dating at the club where Twilight works as an exotic dancer. It's a Gentlemen's Club in Houston I used to go to when I was there on business. One of her benefits working in that club was participating for free when they had speed dating nights. Right, honey?"

Twilight just smiled and leaned her tight body in her even tighter-fitting clothes up against Larry.

I wondered if she had been speed dating after the wedding which might explain the shiner. "Are you from Houston?" I asked Donna.

"Oh no. I just got a job there. I'm from Houma," she said. "You know what they say about Houma—home of oil field trash and proud of it."

Donna was affectionately referring to the area along the southwest corridor from New Orleans to Houston that serviced the oil industry. Many people made a living working offshore on rigs and lived in that area. Many oil companies were headquartered there.

"You said speed dating? Hot dang!" LB said, slapping his hands together. "That's how Julie and me met. Baby, you hear this?" LB called her Julie, not Julia, out loud and right in front of her, even after her brother tried to set him straight. He followed that faux pas up by calling her 'baby' which might make the Choctaw part of her want to scalp him assuming he had any hair under the hat. Again, Julia looked unfazed at the wrong use of her name by her love interest, yet she was shooting daggers at Donna Twilight and Larry.

"Speed dating?" I asked looking at Julia. Something else she failed to mention.

"It's the new way to meet someone and not waste a lot of time with the wrong ones," Larry explained. He popped a bite-sized rum ball into his mouth from the gold foil box Twilight was holding. It looked exactly like the box Jiff and I found in the mailbox that he was still holding.

"Well, we're all for not wasting time to find the right one," Jiff said with his easy charm and quick smile.

Larry was using some sort of twig and spearing two or three rum balls at a time while Donna Twilight held the box. He was raking his teeth along the twig, and at one point he just ate the twig too. Donna Twilight handed him another twig with a rum ball on it. "These are good. Sis, you make em?" he asked Julia. Larry was oblivious to the fact she was trying to ignore him. "I like these here little sticks or twigs you got in 'em. It makes 'em easier to pick up. They're like toothpicks that you can eat." Then he nodded at Jiff holding the gold foil box that looked identical to the one Donna Twilight was holding and said, "You must like 'em too."

Jiff just smiled as we watched Larry go after the rum balls like he was on a strike force. Julia stood studying him a moment before she answered. "No, I did not make any rum balls with twigs in them. None of the boxes I opened had those. Do you remember what box they came out of?"

"Donna, you remember what box had these twigs?" Larry asked his bride. She shook her head no. "Don't know, Sis."

To the rest of us in a nicer tone she said, "Those are all from the Secret Santa exchange we had at my gourmet cooking club. We all had to make our own recipe of rum balls and put them in the same gold box so we wouldn't know who made which one. They are all numbered, and only the president knows whose name is associated with each box. We need to vote on which box we liked best." Back to Larry, and in the not-friendly voice she said, "Could you leave at least one so I can taste it? Don't eat too many or you will ruin your dinner. I went to a lot of trouble to make crown roast."

Jiff had turned over the box of rum balls to see what was on the bottom while Julia was describing the blind taste test. As soon as she finished and before she could lob another insult at Larry, Jiff said, "You know, Julia, something sure smells good."

"That's my crown roast." Julia said. She was all smiles now that Jiff had shifted the attention back to her. She caught Frank's attention and waved him over. "Frank, go check on the crown roast." To the rest of us standing there she said, "Excuse me. I see someone I want to introduce LB to. Dinner should be ready shortly." Julia took LB by the hand to meet the someone across the room.

Larry said to Donna, "Boy, is she gonna have a fit when she finds out we took two boxes with us to the French Quarter." He let out a good-natured laugh. "Baby, didn't those boxes have these twigs in them?"

Donna nodded and held out the box for him to take another rum ball.

"Let's go grab another box of these here rum balls before my sister hides them on me. I saw four or five more boxes in the kitchen." He all but sprinted off in that direction with Donna ambling behind him.

"That crown roast is all she talked about today between yelling at me over the tree lights," Frank said, arriving with more champagne. "She only made it to show off to her gourmet cooking club, not that any one of them would ever give her the satisfaction of telling her it's good. I'm going to have to go help with the food in the kitchen." He pushed the tray of flutes toward us. "Take these last two glasses. I might not be back for awhile."

"Wait, take this box we found left in the mailbox," I said to Frank and put it on his empty tray. "Based on what you told me earlier, it might not be a gift, but it is a box of rum balls."

Jiff said, "You might want to hide any boxes you can find before Larry plunders any more of the rum ball stash." He nodded and took the box Jiff handed him. "Oh, the box we found doesn't have a number on the bottom. Julia said they were all supposed to be numbered."

Frank did one of his signature eye rolls and said as he walked off with the box, "Great. This will make her happy."

"Frank was right," Jiff said. "Larry is definitely in a flop sweat."

"I wonder if he doesn't feel well. I don't think that's normal," I said.

"Hey, they're still on their honeymoon. Maybe they ran upstairs for a quickie," Jiff said.

"Could be," I said. "Donna Twilight has a healthy glow going on too," I said. "Or didn't you notice?"

"I had a hard time noticing anything but her outfit," Jiff said and squeezed my hand.

"Oh, you liked it? Cuz I bought one just like it to wear to your parents' house for Christmas Eve," I tried to say and not laugh.

JIFF AND I roamed around the front two rooms of the double parlor where Julia had the dinner table set and stopped to admire the sideboard arranged with a buffet of cookies, brownies, mini cheesecakes, and every imaginable holiday treat including my favorite, the Kringle. As we moved to the far end of the buffet, Larry and Donna Twilight were arriving at the other end. Larry had another gold foil box and was opening it to see what goodies were inside.

"I love rum balls," he said to no one in particular. "This box don't have them little twigs for toothpicks," he said looking at Twilight.

I noticed he was starting to slur his words and he was sweating more profusely. Twilight retrieved all the toothpick twigs from the box they had left one rum ball in as Julia requested. I figured Twilight learned it was a good idea to keep Larry from getting annoyed. We all wondered if he was the one who gave her the black eye. They both went to the dining room table that was set for twenty people, complete with place cards, and claimed two chairs with table settings side by side. Larry turned the chairs to face one another. It didn't seem to matter, or they didn't notice that neither setting had his or her name on the place card. They proceeded to use the napkins, plates, forks, whatever was in front of them. Julia was not going to like this when it was time for her guests to come into the dining room to be seated and eat. She had gone to a lot of effort to make it a beautifully set table, and it had been until those two sat down.

Larry had another gold foil box that looked like the one we brought in from the mailbox. They put the box of rum balls between them, and Donna started feeding them to Larry between gulps of the whiskey drink Larry had ordered Frank bring to him.

Jiff leaned over my shoulder and whispered in my ear, "See. Larry is romantic."

"Larry is going to be in the hot seat with his sister when Julia sees he wrecked her table settings," I said. We both watched for a brief moment as he practically force-fed Twilight a rum ball she was not interested in eating. When Larry looked around the room, she spit it out in the table napkin. He was spearing two or three at a time and eating them in rapid succession, including the twig toothpicks. Then he and Donna sat with his arm entwined through hers so each of them could drink his or her own drink like you see the bride and groom do at weddings.

"He sure likes rum balls," I said. "You know I make killer ones—I don't care what Julia says about hers. Don't try any of these. I plan to make mine and bring them to your parents' house on Christmas Eve."

"And she cooks!" Jiff said in jest. "My parents are going to be so impressed."

Everyone had congregated to talk and visit in the double parlor across from the dining room, leaving Larry and Twilight sitting at the dining room table set for twenty guests all to themselves. I could see people stick their noses in, spot the two, and walk back to our area.

The house was built in the mid to late eighteen hundred. Julia renovated it into the bed and breakfast keeping the overall design of a center hall with a double parlor, a powder room and staircase on one side, and a long double parlor dining room on the other. The room behind the dining area was a room the gentlemen retired to for a drink or a smoke back in the day. Across the back of the house sat the kitchen with a screened porch off of it. A grand staircase was off to one side in the center hall that led to the guest bedrooms upstairs. Julia had a bedroom and office in one of them. I wondered if Frank moved in and lived here now. He was always at the bed and breakfast when I stopped by.

Jiff and I walked from table to table. Every flat surface inside of the mansion was covered in holiday decor. He finally said, "I thought outdoors was festive. Everything inside looks like outside only in miniature." There were collections of tiny nutcrackers, tiny snowmen, tiny Santa Clauses with and without sleighs or reindeer, doing every conceivable Santa Claus thing. He added, "I counted at least ten tiny nativity scenes. I feel like a motorist passing an accident…and I can't stop looking at it."

Just then there was the sound of flutes and people singing "Deck the Halls" outside. Julia appeared and yelled for Frank in one of her ear-piercing screams while he walked up calmly behind her and stood at her heels. Julia started to say, "Frank, put down those drinks and go get rid of those…"

"I'll do it," I said to cut her off. God knows what Julia would have called them in front of everyone. "Julia, it's the holidays. Be Christian. They are here singing to be nice."

She ignored everything I said after she heard, 'I'll do it.'

Frank followed me to the front door and said, "Be careful and don't let the dogs out. It will be something else I have to do." He slumped his shoulders feigning a look of exhaustion.

Jiff was right behind me when I opened the door just wide enough for both of us to squeeze through. I pulled it closed behind us. We stood in front of the door without our coasts on to hear the singing. Jiff took off his suit jacket and put it around my shoulders. Even if Julia didn't want them gone, I was going to make short work of the entertainment because I was freezing. Julia's dogs were roaming the house and I could hear one or two sniffing and growling on the other side of the door behind me.

It was a nice group of ten or twelve people, all singing from music sheets while one man stood facing them, directing the small choir with his hands. The women all wore period Victorian dresses to their ankles, and the men wore suits, some with velvet vests and top hats. A few had on vintage overcoats with fingerless gloves. Some wore round spectacles sitting on the end of their noses. One man was in a wheelchair with a handmade quilt over his lap, and a lady wearing a bonnet, I assumed she was his wife, stood singing behind him. I smiled and waited until they finished. I started to say, "Thank you. We were just about…" when I was cutoff by an enthusiastic version of "We Wish You a Merry Christmas" before I could finish saying we were about to eat dinner.

What could I do? I didn't want to be rude. I wasn't sure what the proper etiquette was for getting rid of carolers at your front door, or rather someone else's front door. Jiff put his arm around me when he looked over smiling and saw my teeth chattering. Should I invite them in? Julia would probably turn around and shut the door in their faces since it was pretty much the marching order she gave Frank and now expected me to deliver. I was smiling through chattering teeth but contemplating a cutoff tactic while holding the door closed behind me when I felt it yanked out of my hand.

Julia pulled both doors, flinging them open so they were wide apart, letting all the dogs run out at once jumping and howling all over the carolers, especially the man in the wheelchair. I'm sure the six, or maybe it was seven, dogs looked like a rabid pack to the carolers because they did to me. As if on cue from the music director, a terrified look came over their faces and I heard a collective gasp forcing them to lean backwards in unison. They slammed their songbooks shut and took off running in every direction across the lawn, around and over the obstacles as if their lives depended on it. The lady behind the man in the wheelchair threw her songbook in his lap, spun the chair around, and began pushing him as fast as she could across the widest stretch of the front lawn that had a clear view of the street. Since she was the slowest, the dogs were nipping at her heels and barking as if they thought these people were playing a game.

Julia did nothing to call back the dogs. Instead she said to me, "If they knew how much dog poop was in that yard, they wouldn't push a wheelchair that way. C'mon. Let's eat."

She went back inside, calling the other guests to the dining room to eat her crown roast.

Jiff and I watched as most of the carolers made it to the church van parked up the street. Some of the carolers continued to run up the street and the church van followed them, stopping to pick them up. I saw the van following alongside trying to pick up the hysterical woman still running and pushing the wheelchair. I'm surprised no one had a heart attack.

When the dogs got close to the street, they stopped because Julia had a NO FENCE FENCE system. It was an underground circuit that sent a signal to the dogs' collars that shocked them and made them stop when they approached the perimeter of her property where the wire was buried. The dogs knew to stop a few feet from the street. Their barking and howling probably sounded to the carolers like they were still on their heels.

Jiff and I looked at each other when we realized the screaming was coming from the dining room and not the carolers. My first thought was someone knocked the crown roast onto the floor.

Chapter Seven

J IFF GRABBED MY arm and pulled me inside with him to the dining room where we made our way through the bottleneck of people crowded at the door. When we reached the front of all the guests, we saw Larry slumped over in his chair, his face blue and his eyes open. He appeared to have fallen over, planting his face sideways on the table with his eyes wide open and foam coming from his mouth. Twilight had fallen off the chair and was on the floor, not moving, but it looked like she might still be breathing. Jiff rushed to check their pulses, and I saw Julia at the other end of the dining room near the kitchen entrance. She had her hand over her mouth and when she saw me, she started to say, "I can't believe this is happening to me…" and before she said "again" I had pulled her into the kitchen. She was referring to the day she opened her bed and breakfast and a dead guy was found in one of the guest rooms. A dead guy who was the only guest at the time, and the focus of the police investigation had been on Julia.

"Can I please have everyone's attention," Jiff was saying to the guests who were all congested in the wide entry to the dining room off the hall. "This is a crime scene and we all need to sit and wait for the police to get here." Once everyone stepped back, he closed the ten-foot pocket doors that separated the dining room with Larry and Donna in it from the hall and the double parlor where everyone went to wait. LB stayed with Donna, holding her hand.

Jiff came into the kitchen and asked Frank to make sure no one left by the back door. "If they try to leave, get their names." He turned and said to me, "Brandy, take Julia and go to the front. If anyone tries to leave, get his or her name."

"What if they won't tell me their names?" Frank asked.

"Take a picture of them with your cell phone," Jiff said. "I already called 911 for an ambulance."

Most of the guests were agreeable while we waited, and stayed. I sat next to Julia and asked her to help me make a list of the people who were here waiting in case they wanted to leave.

I started on a list of names of the guests I remembered meeting. I counted twenty-one names in all counting Julia, LB, Larry, Donna, Jiff, Frank, and myself. I planned to cross-check them with Frank:

> LB & Julia
> Me and Jiff
> Frank
> Larry and Donna (Twilight)
> Ned and Janice-neighbors across the street
> President of Neighborhood Association & wife – note: wife in Gourmet Club, Ashton and Willa Tripps.
> MacFinns, Sheila and Patrick-Sheila in Gourmet Club & Pilates

<u>Gourmet cooking club ladies' w/spouses:</u>

-Bicky and her husband Matt, last name Favalara—
also in Pilates and cooking
-Lindsay and Lenny something
-Cherie and Dr. Noel St. Pierre

<u>Church Ladies & spouses:</u>
Monica and husband
(Cheryl and Suzette did not attend)

I asked Julia what LB's full name was for the list and where was he from.

"I don't know. I can't think," she said.

"Larry mentioned LB was from Colorado when we all met. Is he?"

"I don't know why Larry said that. He just met LB tonight."

"I wonder how he knew that?" I mused.

"I should've known Larry would screw something up for me tonight," she said.

"What? You think Larry planned to be the dead guy at your party? And Donna? Her new husband is dead and she might not be far behind," I said. "Look over this list of everyone here and see who didn't come."

"Frank is the one who sent out the invites, so he knows who said they were coming and who didn't respond," Julia said.

Right. I should've realized Frank would know more about the people on the list, plus it was hard to get Julia to concentrate.

"Well, let's see. Who might have a grudge against Larry and Donna?" I asked.

"They didn't know anyone here. You knew of them since I told you, but even you never met them before. No one did. Frank never met them before tonight either," she said.

"So, that makes me think you might have been the intended target, or maybe someone spiked those rum balls to make you look bad," I said. While we waited for the ambulance I told her, "Don't you want to get your coat and things so you're ready to go to the hospital with Larry and Donna when the ambulance gets here?"

"Larry is going to the morgue. Everybody can see that," she said.

I was about to ask Julia to tell me about each of the guests on the list when LB pushed open the dining room double doors with one hand while he held the small, limp body of Donna in his arms and said, "We need to get her to an emergency room or she might not make it." He ran to the front door and Jiff opened it and went out with LB to help get Donna into a car. Frank came running with Julia's coat and handbag.

"I don't know Donna that well. Why should I go to the hospital with her?" Julia asked.

I put down the pen on the tablet I was about to take notes on and said, "Maybe because that's your brother in there. That's his wife—your new sister-in-law—and this happened in your house? I think it's your moral duty to follow this through," I said. "Now, go."

She was giving me a look that pretty much suggested I should mind my own business when LB and Jiff ran back in and said to her, "It looks like she's having trouble breathing. We need to get her to an ER now."

"Julia, go with LB and tell him how to get to University Hospital. It's the closest. I'll talk to the police when they get here and tell them where you are," Jiff said.

"Do you mind staying here with Frank tonight?" Then without waiting for my reply, Julia immediately got up and left with LB, while Frank helped her put on her coat as she was being hurried out the door.

While we waited for the police and various departments to arrive in droves, I asked Jiff to wait at the front door while I went to the kitchen to find Frank. I asked him if he had touched all the gold foil boxes that had been delivered so far. He told me yes, and I asked him to work with me and pick up each one and turn it over so I could make a list of the numbers on the bottom. He did. I wrote down the numbers one, four, six and eight. Boxes two, three, five, and seven were missing. The box in the dining room on the table next to the bodies should have had a number, as well as the empty box Larry left on the buffet table.

"Frank, do you know which number was given to Julia for her box of rum balls?" I asked.

"Of course," he said. "She doesn't think I know, but I took the message from the president of the club when she called. I just told her to call her back for her number. She had number three."

"Do you know what boxes Larry and Donna took with them to the French Quarter?"

"No, not really," Frank answered.

If Julia's box three was still here and they took two boxes with them, then the two in the dining room were either two, three, five, or seven. I really hoped Julia's box was not one of the missing two Larry and Donna took to the French Quarter and probably tossed in a trash can. They all needed to be tested.

The ambulance arrived, along with the coroner, the forensics team, and the supporting cast of the police department that are required to come and stampede every crime scene. Especially one that was at a party in a nice big mansion, probably with great food that no one was eating. Cops can find free food faster than they can find a donut shop at break time.

I saw Detective Hanky pull up driving an unmarked police car and double park in the street. She was with a man in plain clothes and I knew it wasn't Dante. He was still in Houston until Christmas Eve or maybe New Year's. Maybe he would stay there forever.

Hanky and Dante were once partners until he was promoted to captain. Now it looked like she had a new partner. A tall, good-looking new partner who had great taste in clothes, even on a policeman's salary.

"Hanky," I said when she and the new guy walked up to Jiff and me waiting on the porch.

The new guy had his shield out and was about to introduce himself when Hanky spoke up, "Brandy Alexander. Jiff Heinkel. This is Detective Travis Taylor. He's new to the city but not new to police work. What have we got here, and please don't tell me Julia is mixed up in murder again."

"Again?" Taylor looked confused.

"Long story, I'll fill you in later," Hanky said and looked at Jiff.

"Right this way. I'll show you what we found when Julia announced that dinner was about to be served," Jiff said, leading the way. Before I followed him, I saw Detective Taylor checking out my cleavage.

Jiff led them to the dining room doorway where he and I stopped. One of the EMTs was listening for a pulse, while the other was administering the paddles to see if they could restart his heart.

"I thought there were two victims here according to the 911 call," Hanky said.

Jiff told Hanky, "Donna was still breathing when we found her, so LB, one of Julia's guests, picked her up and drove her to the emergency room. They left about eight minutes ago. Larry had no pulse and appeared to have expired."

I added, "The man, LB, is not from here and Julia went with them to give directions to University Hospital."

"We weren't in here when they were discovered," Jiff told Hanky and Taylor. "We were outside trying to get the people caroling to leave."

"You wanted people who came caroling to leave?" Detective Taylor asked. He looked perplexed.

"Julia had announced we were about to eat right when the caroling started. Brandy and I went out to see if we could politely send them on their way sooner than later," Jiff explained.

Hanky and Taylor looked at each other and back to the victim while the EMTs tried to resuscitate Larry. The one with the stethoscope put it down and looked at the detectives. He shook his head no.

Taylor asked one of the EMTs if they had any idea on what caused his death when another voice answered.

"Too soon to tell," the voice said as he pushed past us to have a look at Larry's body. He wore a jumpsuit with coroner written in very large letters across the back.

I overheard Detective Taylor ask him, unofficially, if he had any preliminary cause of death. The coroner said the victim showed signs of ingesting poison, but he had no idea which one and wouldn't know until he completed his autopsy report and ran a tox screen.

Jiff and I went into the hall to wait and left the two detectives in the dining room. I started to fill him in on what Frank had told me earlier, adding I had really thought most of it was just crazy stuff, nothing to worry about. He reacted about the rat gift box exactly as I expected.

"I can't believe someone put three rats in a box. One of you could have been really hurt if any of those had bitten you," he said, rubbing my arm as he spoke.

"This is too much to try to focus on in a short period," I said, and listed them. "The rats. The church ladies. The cooking club hostiles. The decoration violations." I had to smile at the last one and so did Jiff. "Frank just dumped so much on me this afternoon and I shrugged it all off. I feel terrible now that this happened."

"How could you know? Frank can be a little theatrical," he said. "You know how Julia was saying all the rum ball boxes had a number on the bottom?"

"Yes, for their blind taste test," I said. "Which really means they came up with that idea so members couldn't rig it to win."

"The box we got out of the mailbox, you know, the one we gave to Frank? It didn't have a number on it," Jiff said.

"Oh boy," I said. "Let me think about this. There's a ninth box. I had Frank turn over the boxes in the kitchen, and I wrote down the numbers. Four numbers were missing. There are two boxes we saw in the dining room. I didn't see the box without a number. I wonder if it's the one in the dining room."

"That will make it difficult to see who sent that one, but not impossible," Jiff said. "It has to be someone on the list of people Julia has ticked off."

"Not a short list, but a list nonetheless," I said.

"You know; I think the coroner is right. Julia's brother and Donna Twilight look like they could have ingested something to poison them. The way he was sweating could mean he started having the effects even before we met him at the party. It could have been something he ate hours ago," Jiff said.

"Frank said or was it Larry who mentioned they took two boxes of rum balls with them when they went down to the French Quarter? When I saw Donna Twilight on the floor, she looked like she was sweating more than she was the last time we saw her. Did you notice?"

"This is above my pay grade, so let's let the police figure this out," Jiff said.

"I don't want to be embroiled in any more of Julia's mess than I have to be, and I don't want you to be sucked in either. I'm glad she has LB to hold her hand because, with the work crunch at the holidays, I don't know how much support or time I can give her," I said.

Hanky asked no one in particular, "You got a cell number for Julia or the guest? We are gonna want to talk to her and the guy who took the woman out of here."

I was in the process of looking up Julia's cell for Hanky when Detective Taylor asked,

"You let her leave?"

No one answered him.

"So. Julia strikes me as the type who would eat her young. You really think she couldn't off her brother and his new wife?" Hanky asked getting out her pen and spiral notebook.

I ignored her. "I made a list of everyone who was here when this happened," I said handing the list to Hanky. I had also made a copy for myself to keep.

Hanky and Taylor looked at the list. Taylor said, "Thank God she didn't have a hundred guests."

Hanky asked Jiff and me, "Can you two answer some questions? Then we'll talk to the others." To Detective Taylor she said, "Take Brandy, but watch out, she's friends with the captain." She winked at me when neither of the men were looking. She asked everyone to wait in the double parlor across from the dining room and then closed those double doors. I would have preferred to talk with her as we had worked together in the past, and she knew I could be helpful. She walked to the far end of the hall to speak with Jiff, leaving me alone with Detective Taylor. Taylor was going to take some training.

"So you know Captain Deedler?" Taylor asked.

"Yes," I said. "So you're Hanky's new partner? Permanent?"

"Yeah. It looks permanent. Captain Deedler is in Houston for a mandatory police conference. All the captains and the chief of detectives had to attend."

"I know," I said. I left off the part where I just found out this afternoon.

"How well do you know Captain Deedler?" Taylor was trying to read my responses.

"I'll give you a hint since you're new. We grew up next door to each other, and my sister married one of his brothers."

"Okay. Got it." He opened a notebook and said, "State your full name, please."

"Brandy. Brandy Alexander," I said. "Before you ask Detective Newbie, it is not a stage name and I don't work on Bourbon Street," I told him. I folded my arms across my chest until I realized it made my boobs looks like they were going to pop out of my top, so I put my arms at my sides.

"Is it Miss, Mrs., or Ms. Brandy, Brandy Alexander? Two first names, right?"

"That's Ms." I didn't answer the other one and I tried not to smile. It would only encourage him if he thought he made me laugh.

"Oh, you're *that* Brandy Alexander," he said, nodding like he'd just made some mystic connection. He looked up and said, "Don't you date Captain…"

I cut him off, "Don't go there," I said. "Please."

"So, what brings you here tonight?" Detective Taylor asked.

"It's a party." I opened my eyes wide and held my hands out even wider to make the point. I added, "I was invited. And now, since there's a dead person here, you've been invited." I fought the urge to smile but failed.

"Yes. It's a party when the police arrive," he added, and I could see he found it amusing too.

Not only was he tall, but he was also fit. He looked like he worked out at a gym regularly. He had blondish hair cut short and spiked with gel on top. He started to remove his very nice overcoat, the long kind you see people in colder climates wear. He was about to put it on a chair, but I reached for it and offered to hold it for him.

He thanked me and said how warm it was inside. *Warm inside?* The doors had been wide open since the arrival of the EMTs, the police, and forensic team, so inside now felt like outside. I considered putting my own coat on. Where was this guy from—Alaska?

When I touched his coat, I realized it was cashmere. Nice. The suit he had on was an expensive one. I thought, *I bet they paid a lot better wherever he came from than the police department is going to pay him here.*

"Here, let me put that around your shoulders," Taylor said when he saw me roll my hands in his coat to keep them warm or maybe it was the sound of my teeth chattering that made him take notice.

"Thanks," I said as he draped his coat over me.

"How do you know the victims?" he asked.

"I never met them before tonight. I only knew Julia had a brother named Larry. This is Julia's house and she is hosting this party. Her name is Julia Richard. His name is Larry Richard."

"How do you spell that last name?"

"It's spelled like the man's name, Richard, but it's French, Reee…chard," I said to exaggerate the pronunciation.

"What can you tell me about the woman victim?" he asked.

"I met both victims about forty minutes ago. The woman introduced herself as Donna with a stage name of Twilight," I said. "She had a black eye."

Taylor kept writing but lifted his eyebrows at the mention of the shiner.

"Anything else?" he asked.

"All I know about him is what Julia has told me. Julia said her brother lived in Baton Rouge but worked the oil industry from New Orleans to Houston. When we were all introduced, Larry introduced the woman as Donna, his new wife of two weeks. I heard him tell someone else they met speed dating in Houston."

"Is that it?" Taylor asked.

"I saw them sitting at the dining room table eating rum balls," I said. "And then the next time I saw them; they were still in the dining room. Larry was slumped over on the table and she was on the floor. Larry looked, well, he looked dead. She was barely breathing, or so it seemed to me. I guess that's why LB grabbed her and took her to the hospital."

"LB?"

"All I know about LB is Julia met him speed dating a couple of weeks ago and has been seeing him since. I also met him for the first time tonight at this party so I can't tell you much about him either," I said.

"Do you know anyone here that would want to see Larry and his new wife dead?"

I immediately thought Julia might but I shook my head no. I said, "You know he was eating rum balls that were left here as part of a Secret Santa gift exchange for Julia's cooking club. I think something might be in one of those boxes. Larry had been eating those like there's no tomorrow. I saw him force one on his wife and when he wasn't looking, I saw her spit it out in a napkin. The rest of the boxes are in the kitchen."

"Good, thanks for telling me," he said. "We'll also take those boxes with us for forensics to run their tests on. Please show me where you think they all are."

He had an accent which was definitely not a New Orleans one but close. Then I realized he was a New Yorker.

"There are boxes in the kitchen and two in the dining room," I said.

Taylor called a forensic technician over and told him to gather the gold foiled boxes of rum balls in the dining room and kitchen for evidence.

"Who else do you know here?" Detective Travis Taylor asked me.

"I really only knew two of the other guests here tonight. They are neighbors Ned and Janice who live directly across the street. They adopted one of my rescued dogs about a year ago, but that was the last time I saw them before tonight. I know Julia, the woman who lives here and owns the bed and breakfast, Jiff Heinkel, and Frank. Everyone else I met for the first time tonight. I did meet LB, Julia's new boyfriend, when he answered the door. I never saw or met him before this party."

"How do you know Julia Richard?" He said it like the man's name.

"Julia Richard…" I pronounced it properly in French, "and we know each other from where we were both previously employed. I met her about three years ago, and we have stayed in contact even after the company downsized and she was let go. I still work there. In fact, she asked me to stay here tonight with Frank."

"Who's Frank? Your boyfriend?" he asked while making notes, but I saw him look up to see how I reacted.

"I'm guessing you haven't met Frank yet. Frank is the waiter and bartender tonight. He works here."

"Oh, that guy." He looked at me somewhat amused and asked, "How do you know Frank? The waiter?"

Something in the way Detective Travis Taylor was watching me when he asked me the question made me feel uncomfortable. He wasn't looking me up and down, but his eyes were dark, almost black, and he was watching me with a little too much intensity causing me to feel self-conscious when I answered a question.

"Frank is not a waiter. Well, he's the waiter tonight. Frank is Julia's handyman here at the bed and breakfast. Well, he's not really a handyman. Frank is more of an interior designer and makes Julia's clothes. He sews and handles her social responses. He's more of a personal assistant." I stopped talking because Detective Taylor stopped writing and stood looking at me while I rattled on about Frank.

"So, Frank, the waiter, is only a waiter tonight because he is not really a handyman, but rather a seamstress, an interior decorator, and a personal assistant? Frank has a big job description and more responsibilities than the President of the United States."

"You know what? You can figure it out, Mr. Oh-So-Smart Detective not from here. I'm trying to tell you who he is and how he fits in around here with Julia so you can see he's not a suspect," I said feeling very protective of Frank.

"How does Julia know Frank besides his renaissance ability to be everyman?" he asked.

I stood trying to figure out how to answer this without incriminating Frank and Julia. He asked questions in a way that wasn't rude, just overt.

"I think you should ask them," I said.

"I'm asking you. If you know, please tell me." He waited with his ink pen, I then noticed to be a Mont Blanc, poised over his rather nice, leather-bound notepad. Actually, it was a leather cover that a spiral notepad could be slipped into and replaced as needed. It covered the notepad and tied closed.

I let out a big breath. This was going to make his day. "Julia met Frank in central lockup when she was arrested for murdering a guest here in the bed and breakfast. You could probably get that exact date from the police reports that were filed. Ask Hanky. She worked that case and will remember. Will there be anything else?" I asked.

"Yeah. One more thing. Who was the guy standing with you when Detective Hanky and I pulled up?"

"Jiff Heinkel."

"How do you know him?"

"I already mentioned he's the only other person I know here tonight. He is my escort to this party," I answered. Calling someone my boyfriend sounds like high school and saying he was my significant other suggested we are living together. Calling him my date implies a casual, not an ongoing relationship. Jiff was none of the above.

"Escort as in date, friend, or as in paid?" He had a deadpan look on his face.

"Are you asking if I'm his paid escort or if he is mine?"

"Escort can go a lot of different ways. I've only been here six weeks. Everything about this city is new to me. You guys have weird names and do weird things, and most of the time it sounds like you are speaking a foreign language. I'm just trying to get the correct information."

Yeah right. I crossed my arms across my chest. I felt my chin push up toward the ceiling.

"Please, just one more thing. What's the fascination with costumes and big, plastic blow-up Christmas objects on the front lawns here? I saw a big, pink pig dressed up like Santa Claus."

"That's just normal stuff," I said.

"Since I've been here I haven't seen anything that comes close to normal," he said.

"So what *did* bring you here from New York?" A quick eye movement showed an instant of surprise that I guessed where he was from.

"I worked ten years in homicide and undercover there, and I saw too many weird and strange people do too many weird and strange things. I wanted to get away from it," he said.

"You moved to New Orleans to get away from weird and strange? We wrote the book on weird and strange. Wait until Mardi Gras." This guy didn't know what he was in for. I felt myself smiling because I felt sorry for him. "Are we finished Detective?"

"Well, I finally got you to smile. Thank you, Ms. Brandy, Brandy Alexander. I'm sure I'll want to speak with you again." I could feel him watching me walk away from him.

Chapter Eight

F RANK LOOKED RELIEVED when I said I'd stay the night, because Julia had called and said she would be home really late if at all. He found me some night clothes and set up one of the upstairs guest rooms for me.

"Frank, why isn't she staying the night at the hotel with LB?" I asked. "He said he was staying at the Fairmont. That's just a block or so away."

"I asked her that, and she said she didn't have a change of clothes. You know Miss Priss wants to look like a million bucks when she steps out of here," he said. "Besides, she thinks he has money and she wants to make sure before she jumps in bed with him. She thinks it makes her more desirable." Frank did his signature eye roll.

Jiff and I decided it might be best if I stayed and he would come get me tomorrow. It was late, almost 3:00 am I had already called my roommate, Suzanne, and asked if she would take care of my dog, Meaux. I kissed Jiff good night, and I went back to the kitchen. Frank was busy cleaning up and putting away dishes, covering leftovers, and sampling things here and there before he wrapped them up and put them in the refrigerator. He pulled out two clean plates, set them on the kitchen island, and then pulled two ribs off the crown roast and put one on each plate.

"Might as well see if this is as good as she said it was going to be." He cut off a big bite and after taking a moment to make a decision, started shaking his head yes and making an um-m-m sound.

I tried my piece by taking a tiny nibble off the bone and Frank was right, it was tasty. The presentation was pretty with all the ribs in a circle with the ends sticking up. Each rib was wearing a small white topper that looked like tiny chefs' hats. After we ate our helping of dinner, we both were ready for bed. It was almost 3:30 a.m. when Frank finished cleaning up and putting things away in the refrigerator. Eating made me even more sleepy.

Before my eyes closed I asked Frank, "What inheritance were you talking about with Julia and her brother earlier. We got cut off."

"She got a call from an attorney a couple of weeks ago, and he told her that her dad had died and left no will, so it was going to probate. I don't know what that means, but her dad's estate was worth a lot of money, and it would go to her and her brother," Frank said.

"Do you know how much?" I asked him.

"No, I went to listen in on her office extension, but by the time I got there to pick up, I guess the attorney had already told her," Frank said and was about to continue.

"Frank, you eavesdrop on her calls?" I asked.

"Of course, how else do you think I know what goes on around here. Anyway, as I was saying… she was asking the attorney not to tell her brother until she had a chance to speak with him. The attorney said it was too late, Larry already knew," he said.

"I'm exhausted, Frank. I hope money is not at the bottom of all this between Julia and her brother. Let's talk about this some more in the morning if Julia isn't home," I said and headed upstairs.

In one of the vacant guest rooms, there was a warm up-suit of Julia's Frank put on the bed for me to sleep in. Tomorrow I'd just have to wear the warm up home and pull my hair into a ponytail. I started to doze off and boxes of rum balls danced in my head. My eyes popped open when the one from the mailbox danced by. Who sent those rum balls? It was the only thing Larry was eating, and eating a lot of. It had to be the rum balls, and Julia said they were all anonymous except that the president of the gourmet club knew who sent which one. Maybe someone sent an extra.

Every time I dozed off another question I needed to know the answer to would pop in my head. So much didn't add up, and I needed some basic info from Julia or Frank. I thought maybe someone who wasn't at the party might be important, like the someone who might be in the gourmet club that might have left the gift in the mailbox.

By 7:00 a.m. I was sitting in the kitchen having a cup of coffee. No one else seemed to be stirring. All the dogs were put on the back porch at night. I looked in on them trying to decide if I should let them out, but they all were zonked out asleep. They hadn't recovered from the late night either.

I sat down with the list of people Julia and I had made while we waited for the police. Frank and Julia would have to help me fill it in. I started making notes to keep me on track, because once Frank and Julia started to tag team me, I might run up the street screaming. It's a good thing this was a Saturday and Christmas Eve was a week away. I still had some shopping to do and gifts to wrap. Work had not slowed down, and there were a couple of things I had to do before I closed out the year. Jiff and I had a full week of night or evening activities planned. There was Christmas Caroling in Jackson Square tomorrow night. Tonight was a Holiday Yappy Hour where we could have photos taken with our pets. My place of employment had an after work get together one night this week and so did Jiff's office. I still had to get a gift for Jiff's parents since we were spending Christmas Eve with them. I added it to my Christmas to-do list in between jotting down questions for Julia and Frank.

I was tapping my pen on the list of people, trying to think of what didn't add up. If the rum balls were poisoned or tampered with, that would be figured out fast enough by the police. Then the president of the gourmet cooking club would find whose name was associated with that box number and case closed.

The holidays would resume for everyone except Donna, if she made it, and Julia, who would have to bury her brother. The police needed to find the murderer. Twenty-one people were here, and the only ones I was certain were not the killers were Jiff and myself. While the two neighbors I knew didn't seem like they would murder anyone or have a reason to, I wouldn't put my neck on the chopping block for Janice. She had Julia issues too.

While I waited for Frank to wake up, I called and spoke to Suzanne, "Hey, I'm sorry to have to ask you again, would you mind feeding Meaux this morning and letting him out and back in? I'll be home in a couple of hours… I hope."

"I already fed him and I let him sleep with me last night. How's it going over there? Do you want me to come rescue you from the clutches of Julia's weird and strange world?" *Weird and strange.* I thought about the conversation with Detective Taylor last night.

"No. Jiff will come get me or I'll grab a cab. It wasn't the party we thought we were going to, that's for sure. Be glad you didn't come. Although… since someone left a box of rum balls anonymously, and we think that might be what killed Larry and made Donna sick, I'll have to add you to the suspect list," I joked.

"If I had any free time between work, school, and studying, and I wanted to kill Julia, I wouldn't waste any of it making something for her to eat and hope she eats it. I'd just knock her in the head," Suzanne said. "Besides, I was working last night."

"Yes, that's a good alibi only if your work confirms it. Then your statement clears you," I continued to joke with her. "You are more action oriented. Believe me, there are enough suspects right now without trying to find more. Tell Meaux I'll be home as soon as I can."

"You really need to consider Frank as the murderer. If I had to work with Julia as much as he does, I would have tried to kill her by now. Maybe his attempt went haywire. Don't overlook the obvious," Suzanne said laughing. She added, "Don't worry, your precious Meaux will still love you when you get home, even though I am making inroads to displace you with food. See you later."

Hanky had left a message on my cell phone. She and Taylor had gone to the hospital and said the doctors were cautiously optimistic that Donna might pull through. Julia's brother arrived DOA. The coroner still had to do an autopsy but should get the tox screen back soon. His initial findings looked like poison. After all the tests results came back they would know more.

Frank drifted down first around 9:15 a.m. He isn't a morning person, so I was surprised he was up before noon.

"Some night, huh?" I greeted him. "Not the party I was expecting."

"Not a party. She will be tougher than usual to deal with today." Frank looked at me and said, "You sure you want to be here when she gets back, cuz I know I would rather be somewhere else. I have to be here. You can leave."

While Frank and I were alone in the kitchen, I asked, "What do you think of Julia's new boyfriend, LB?" Even though Julia was not here, she had an unbelievable ability to overhear a whisper across a street while she stood next to a jackhammer. I worried she could somehow hear us talking right now from wherever she was.

"Hmmm," Frank slowed his movements in mid dishwasher unloading to choose his words. "He seems all right at first, but then he gets pushy," he said.

"What do you mean 'he gets pushy?'" I asked him. "How so?"

"Well, like yesterday when Julia's brother and the wife arrived early, she sent them off to the French Quarter, remember? Well, they left their luggage inside in the hallway. When LB came over and saw it there he told me, didn't ask mind you, told me to bring their luggage upstairs and put it in their rooms," Frank said. "It was like he knew who it belonged to without asking."

I raised an eyebrow, thinking most luggage was bigger than Frank, and there was no elevator in here. I couldn't imagine elfin Frank wrestling a big rolling bag up the grand staircase, just like I couldn't imagine him setting up the nutcrackers on either side of the entry doors. "So what did you do?" I asked him.

"Julia heard him and said Larry could drag his bags and Donna's upstairs himself. 'LB,' she said, 'I have Frank doing things here to help me for this party tonight. If you want those bags upstairs, you can take them yourself.'" Frank's hands had started shaking, and he almost dropped a plate.

"What is it, Frank?" I asked and took the plate from him, closing the dishwasher door. "What is it about him?"

"He gave me a sideways look that was so mean, like he was not used to someone not jumping to do what he told that someone to do," Frank said.

"Well, Julia was the one who told him she didn't want you doing that," I said.

"Yeah, but I got the feeling from the look he gave me that he expected me to do it anyway. He's weird," Frank said.

"Weird and strange?" I asked. I really thought about doing a list of everyone ever referred to as weird and strange and comparing all the names to each other to see what made them similar.

"No, weird and mean," Frank said. "I've met men like him before. He appears to Julia all nice and helpful, but I don't trust him. She doesn't really know him, and everything she knows about him, he told her."

"What did he tell her about himself? Rather, what has she told you she knows about him?" I asked.

"I think she said his last name was Smith or maybe it was Sutton. Sutton. It's Sutton. Before you ask, I don't know what LB stands for," Frank said, opening the dishwasher door to finish unloading it. "Julia and Larry are from Baton Rouge and sound like they're from Texas. I'm guessing he's from Texas, too, since he wears that big hat." Frank was running his fingers through his pixie haircut in an attempt to get it to wisp along his face. He went to the kitchen sink and wet his fingers to help his hair cooperate, and I noticed his hands were still shaking.

"Do you know what he does?" I asked. "That bracelet he gave Julia had to set him back a bit."

"If it's real," Frank said. "I don't know what he does, and I don't think the Queen does either or she'd be all over repeating it a hundred times like the crown roast," Frank said looking at his reflection in the stainless toaster. He was licking his fingers and running them along his eyebrows. "She wants me to call the insurance company today and add the bracelet under her policy." He let out a sigh as if a phone call would tax him terribly.

"That roast was good, so she had a right to brag on it," I said.

"I'm sure we will hear it again today after she has a serving," Frank said as he was checking his eyebrows in his toaster reflection again.

"You said he's staying at the Fairmont. That's close to the hospital," I said.

"He likes the lobby. Probably because it's the only place in the city with as many Christmas decorations as here," Frank said. He was putting out a clean cup and saucer for my coffee and fumbled, breaking the cup. I watched his hands shaking as he cleaned up the pieces.

"I don't need another cup, Frank. I'm good with this one," I said.

"LB called and said he's bringing Julia home this morning and then he's going back to the hospital to sit with Donna."

"That's nice of him," I said.

"Nice? I think it's weird," Frank said. "LB doesn't know Donna. He's here to see Julia and he's willing to sit in a hospital room for hours waiting for Donna to wake up?" Frank said. "Why?"

"Maybe he's trying to impress Julia, or she sees something in him we don't," I said.

"Julia wants to see something in him. She wants what you have," Frank said.

"What I have? What do I have that Julia doesn't have ten times, if not," I waved my hands around to indicate the mansion, "one hundred times more of?"

"Well, you have Jiff who is over the moon for you," Frank said, stopping whatever he was fussing with and looking square at me. "And, you have Dante who you are over the moon for. Julia wants those things. Oh wait, someone is over the moon for her. It's Julia who is over the moon for herself. My bad."

"Frank, be nice to me or I might have to tell her you said that," I said while a big smile forced its way on my face.

"Frank do you remember anything you didn't mention to the police about last night—the guests, the neighbors, the rum balls—anything?"

He started to say no but stopped. "This might be nothing, but when Julia isn't home, LB stops by and I can hear him walking all over upstairs, snooping from room to room. I think he's looking for something."

"That's a little forward. Did you ever hear him say where he's from?" I asked. "I heard Larry ask LB if everyone wore hats like his in Colorado. How did Larry know he was from Colorado?"

"No idea," Frank answered.

"LB hasn't known Julia that long, has he?" I asked.

"Maybe two to three weeks," Frank said. "She and Larry have that in common. He married Donna two weeks ago. I don't think they had a long love affair either."

"That's right," I said. "Well, maybe they both wanted someone in their lives since their dad just died not long ago. Maybe they felt the need for family when their last parent died."

"I think it has more to do with the dad's inheritance. I heard Julia on the phone with an attorney, and she asked what did her brother know about it. And that was before she knew he got married," Frank said.

"What about Larry and Donna? Were you here when they arrived?"

"Yes, they got here right after you left. She sent them to the French Quarter pronto. The only thing I remember about them is he was sweating when he came back here, and it kept getting worse from there. I don't remember him sweating like that before he left. Julia even commented on it, or rather commanded him to change his shirt before the party," Frank said.

"Did he? Did he change his shirt?" I asked.

"Yes, for all the good it did," Frank said. "LB got here right after they left. That's when he told me to take up the luggage."

"So, LB met Larry and Donna when they came back here from the French Quarter?"

"No, he had left by then to go back to his hotel to change. He came back before Larry and Donna came downstairs to join the party. They came down right after you arrived," Frank said, striking his thinking pose of one hand holding his elbow while the other hand held a finger to his lips.

Hmm. I wonder why Larry thought LB was from Colorado, I thought to myself. I asked Frank, "What did the police ask you, and what did you tell them?"

Frank's hands started to shake again and he said, "That new cop, Detective Taylor, he called me a jailbird." He asked me, 'What's a jailbird like you doing in a nice place like this?'"

"Frank, you know those cops all act like everyone is guilty. Besides, he's new here. Hanky will set him straight," I said.

"They both think I did it. Detective Hanky doesn't like me and she doesn't like Julia. She told Detective Taylor I was an ex-con, and I was probably here trying to rob Julia and her guests," he said, barely getting the words out before he started crying. "I'm not an ex-con," he blubbered. "I spent one night in Central Lockup because some drunken tourist in the French Quarter said I was trying to steal the broach off the jacket she was wearing. I was just admiring it."

"Frank, we need your help, so pull yourself together. Besides, you know Julia and I don't think that, and we know that's not what happened, so let's try and figure out what did happen yesterday," I said. "You know more about the goings on around here than Julia does. Did you tell the police about the rats?"

"No, I didn't, and I don't really want to. No one saw that except me," he said.

"And me," I said.

"Did you give them the boxes of rum balls?" I asked him. "I told Detective Taylor I saw two empty boxes in the dining room and there were more in the kitchen."

"Yes, and Detective Taylor asked me if I touched them. Of course I touched them. They didn't walk into the kitchen by themselves," he said.

"That's just so they know whose fingerprints to eliminate if they dust for them," I told Frank. "By the way, do you have a phone number for the president of the cooking club?"

"Yes, I'll get it for you. Why are you calling her?" Frank asked. "She's like ninety years old. She told me she started this club over fifty years ago. She never comes to the meetings or cooking classes anymore, but she likes to stay involved."

"I want to ask her who had what number she assigned to the rum ball boxes," I said.

"Well, you might want to go see her. She might be losing her hearing. Julia screams at her over the phone when she calls her," Frank said.

Just then we heard Julia come in through the front door.

"Oh, wow," I said. "I thought you came back late last night and were upstairs sleeping."

"The doctor just gave us an update about an hour ago. I'm just getting home," she said.

"You didn't want to stay downtown with LB?" I asked.

"I've got a lot to do, and sitting around in the hospital waiting on someone to wake up is not a good use of my time. LB brought me home and went back to wait there with Donna," she said, going for a cup of coffee.

"That's nice of him to wait, so if she wakes up she sees a familiar face," Frank said and gave me a quick look when he was sure Julia wouldn't see it.

"How familiar is LB with Donna? Didn't she just meet him at the party?" I asked. "Do you think he's the right person for her to see when she wakes up?"

"Yeah," Julia answered. "LB just met Larry and Donna last night. LB being there when she wakes up is better than no one being there, and a hundred times better than me having to be there."

This was odd. Julia didn't seem worried about her new man sitting at a hospital waiting for a woman he didn't know to wake up.

I asked Julia, "How did you meet LB? He said ya'll met speed dating?"

Frank got up to make another pot of coffee.

Julia crossed her arms over her chest and said, "He's a nice, older man, and we met in a bar where there was speed dating when I went there to sign up. Once we started talking over drinks, we decided to go have dinner instead. LB just likes saying that. What's wrong with speed dating anyway?"

"Nothing's wrong with speed dating, I guess. I don't know much about it. What else do you know about LB?" I asked.

Julia arms were still crossed over her chest, and now she pushed back her chair and crossed her legs. Frank was standing behind Julia, giving me the knife across the throat move suggesting I stop with the questions. Something was off, but I couldn't put my finger on it. Then she jumped up to get the coffee Frank was already trying to pour for her. She startled him, and he almost dropped the coffee pot.

"I need my coffee, Frank," she snapped and sat back down. Frank hustled over and fawned over her from side to side, setting a cup, saucer, spoon, and linen napkin in front of her. Then he put out the creamer and sugar holder and brought the coffee pot to the table. He placed it on a metal table protector he put down first. He poured her a cup and then put the pot on the protector and covered the pot with a quilted cozy cover. I thought he was setting the table for the Royal Tea.

"Are we expecting the Queen of England?" I asked, trying to infuse some humor and lighten the mood. Neither one of them found it funny. "Larry said LB was from Colorado. Is he here on business or just visiting? He must be crazy about you since I saw that bracelet he gave you," I said, trying to tone down the inquisition. Frank was standing behind Julia rolling his eyes.

"He told me he manages his family's businesses all over the country. He can afford to give expensive things," Julia said without elaboration. I waited for a Julia rant with the usual outpour of needless information, but none came.

"I'm sure he can, but isn't this a little early in your relationship? I mean how long have you known him? How long has he been here?" I asked.

"Why? What do you think is so wrong with him?" Julia stood with her her arms crossed over her chest and was waiting for an answer from me.

Red flag. Frank was doing the throat cutting maneuver again, so I changed my approach and said, "I don't think anything is wrong with him. I was trying to find out about your new guy. You know how we are here in New Orleans. You've lived here long enough. We want to figure out who he knows that we might know. I'm looking out for you. I'm sorry if you find that upsetting."

"I can worry about myself, thank you very much," Julia said.

I thought with all the Christmas shopping I still had to do, my time would be better spent getting items done on that list. I decided to come back tomorrow or in a day or two after Julia had more sleep. She was crabby when she was tired and last night's events made her more so.

"Uber is picking me up in a few minutes, so let me go get my things. Can I get this warm-up suit back to you later?" I asked.

Julia nodded yes with her arms still folded across her chest. Frank followed me upstairs. I asked him to find out what he could on LB if he came back. "See if you can get a look at his last name on his driver's license. I wonder if his name is really Sutton," I said.

Chapter Nine

I LIVED JUST a short uber ride home from Julia. It was great to walk through my door, even if Suzanne wasn't home, because Meaux was so excited to see me. We played a bit before I heard a knock on our front door. I answered it to find Detective Hanky standing on my front porch.

"Hanky, where's your sidekick? Here alone?" I asked.

"You're wanting to know where Detective Taylor is?" she asked.

"No. I thought you always travel in pairs. You and Dante were always together," I said. "Or so it seemed."

"I told you he was on the fast track and he wouldn't be a detective forever," she said.

"Yes, but now I bet he's working even more, longer hours with more responsibility. So, Taylor looks like your new partner."

"Are you sweet on him? That's the second time in under a minute you asked about him." Hanky said.

"Oh, that's right. You are a detective. Good with math too, I see," I said shrugging her off.

"Do you want me to tell him you like him?" Hanky pressed, trying to get a reaction.

"Are you trying to make my life more difficult than it has to be? Why don't you point him in Julia's direction? She needs a man," I said. "Maybe they would be good for each other."

"Taylor is a Yankee, but that's no reason to throw him under the Julia bus. There isn't a man on this planet that Julia will find perfect enough for her or one that I dislike enough to set her up with," Hanky said. "The next serial killer I arrest, I'll suggest he give Julia a call."

"Here you are, sugarcoating everything again. Just tell me how you really feel about Julia," I said, laughing at her. "I'm trying to help Julia out. She tried a dating service. That went nowhere," I said. "Look at ten-gallon hat. Julia likes him and it looks like he likes her."

"About that," Hanky said, taking out her notepad. "Taylor and I went to talk to the two of them, but LB wasn't there and Atom Ant, I mean Frank, said Julia had just gotten home from spending all night at the hospital and was upstairs sleeping. I sent Taylor to the hospital to talk to Julia's boyfriend, this LB. You were at the party, what do you know about him?"

"Not much. We said hello at the door. We didn't really chat. We overheard him talking to others, but it was all small talk, chit chat. Julia's being tight-lipped which is unusual for her when she's got a good thing going. Even Frank doesn't seem to know much about him. You know Frank eavesdrops on Julia, right? He always knows more than you think he does," I said.

"That little putz," Hanky said.

"Don't tell him I told you, but keep it in your back pocket. He knows and sees more than Julia does," I said. "I got the feeling Frank is wary of LB too. I laid eyes on him for the first time last night, just a couple of hours before you did. I heard him tell Larry that he met Julia speed dating. She didn't really deny it," I said. "Oh, and he calls her Julie not Julia. Doesn't seem like he's making much of an effort with Julia, but did you see that bracelet he gave her?"

"What's speed dating? Do you think I should try it?" she asked.

I explained to her the concept of speed dating. Then I asked Hanky, "Would you leave your gun home if you went speed dating?"

"No."

"Then speed dating is not for you," I said. "You meet men in a short amount of time. Sounds good, right? Except it would make you want to shoot them."

Hanky had been raised by a single parent—her cop father. She did what he did, and he didn't do girly things so neither did Hanky. She wasn't a tomboy. She just didn't know what makeup to use or what clothes to wear to make herself attractive. After I gave her a makeover a few months ago, men started to notice and flirt with her. She was beginning to enjoy the attention but hadn't started dating anyone in particular. While we often commiserated that we didn't understand men, Hanky said she just wished she could shoot them. I figured speed dating would only make Hanky want to shoot more men faster.

I filled her in on what Julia told us when she went to sign up. "She said she got cold feet and went for a drink at the bar. He was there at the bar waiting for the speed-dating bell to ring. After they started talking, they both decided to blow off the dating fiasco and go somewhere for dinner," I said.

"She went off with a stranger she just met in a bar? What's wrong with her?" Hanky asked. "Does she ever watch the news?"

"What's he doing here speed dating if he's visiting from Colorado?" I said.

"That's a good question, and Julia should have asked him. We'll have to ask her," Hanky said. "Taylor went to the Fairmont to interview LB. We called, and Frank said that's where he's staying. I wonder why he's not staying with Julia. Do you want to go with me to see her?"

"We?" I mocked. "Does that mean you're dumping your partner, His Gucci-ness—Detective Taylor, for me? What's the scoop on him anyway?" I asked. "He told me he worked ten years in New York."

"He's a little different," Hanky said. "He does dress much nicer than the other guys. Some have been ribbing him over it. If he asks a question, one of these goofballs will say, 'Why don't you ask your Rubenstein Brothers?'"

Rubenstein Brothers was a high-end clothing store for men that has been in New Orleans on prestigious St. Charles Avenue and the corner of Canal Street for almost one hundred years. Everyone's father, grandfather, or great-grandfather probably had at least one suit from Rubenstein Brothers back in his day.

I said, "He told me he saw too much weird and strange in New York. That's why he said he left there. There's something about him that doesn't track with undercover work. It's more like he went to Detective Finishing School than Tattoos R Us."

That made Hanky laugh. "Undercover? Is that what he told you? I guess technically he was, just not street level…

more penthouse-view undercover. He worked high-end crimes. You know. the international playboy types with lots of money who were doing some really bad-boy things like human trafficking, arms dealers, child porn. So far, Taylor's all right for the most part," Hanky said. "His own car is a big Mercedes, and check out the suits he wears. I can tell you he doesn't shop at Men's Wearhouse like the rest of the guys in the department. The guy's smart and classy. He could give your Mr. Hottie a run for his money."

"I don't think so. Let's point him in Julia's direction, but she isn't going to go for anyone she thinks lives on a cop's salary. Sorry, but that's one thing she ragged on me about when I was dating Dante."

"When you *were* dating? When did you stop dating Dante?" Hanky looked confused.

"That's over. It's been over and neither one of us wants to admit it," I said.

"You need to tell him. Dante made a comment about going to some family party with you before he left for Houston," Hanky said.

"Really? To date, you must communicate. He must be in denial. That's what you call it when one of you thinks you're dating and the other one doesn't. We haven't made any plans because I haven't heard from him in weeks," I said. "It's the holidays and Christmas is a week away. How could he possibly think he can just call me up now and pick up where we left off? If he can't remember the last time we communicated, then he needs a time management course."

Hanky shrugged. She probably knew Dante as well as or better than I did. They worked as partners, and she at least had a front row seat when it came to seeing how he thinks.

I had to ask her, "What did you tell your new partner about me and Dante?"

"I told him you two have history, that's all. I think he was curious to see if you were available since you were there with another guy."

"I'd have to be out of my mind to date another policeman, let alone someone who works for Dante," I said.

"Not out of your mind, more like you have a death wish for the other cop," Hanky said with a mischievous grin. "Let's go talk to Julia and Frank. I want to see if anyone remembers anything else from last night."

"Maybe you'll have better luck than I did this morning," I said. "Julia had been up all night at the hospital and she was crabby."

"Take a ride with me. She ought to be awake by now. I'll have you back here in an hour," Hanky said.

"I can't go back there today. I have too much to do, but I can go with you tomorrow. There's a ton of last-minute stuff I need to do before I go to Yappy Hour with Jiff and Meaux. Meaux needs to go see the groomer so he will be handsome for the paw-ty photos. Jiff's bringing Isabella. You can have photos taken with Santa Paws and your pets for a donation."

"If I get off early enough I'll come and bring Valentine," she said. Hanky had adopted a schnauzer from me a few months back. "I really want you there when I question Frank and Julia, because you know those two and you'll know if they're holding back. Let's go tomorrow, say 10:00 a.m.?"

"Make it 1:00 o'clock if you want them up and awake," I said. "The guest house is vacant for the holidays so they both sleep late. Hey, did anything come back on the boxes of rum balls yet?"

"No, maybe tomorrow we'll know something from the tox screen. See you at one tomorrow," Hanky said. "I'll swing by and pick you up. You can ride with me if Taylor's not going, or you can follow in your car." Hanky left and I went back to getting my things together for the hectic day I had ahead of me.

Y Y Y

JIFF ARRIVED WITH his dog Isabella to pick us up that afternoon at five-thirty. Isabella looked recently groomed.

"Well, don't you look pretty, Miss Isabella?" I said petting her. "Meaux went to the stylist today so he would look handsome for his Santa photo with you." I had made a red-plaid vest and bought a red-knit scarf from the pet boutique for him to wear in the photos. He would stand out against the off-white beaded sweater I wore over cream colored pants. I made the same red-plaid vest, only a little longer with a ruffle around the neck, for Isabella so she looked more like she was wearing a dress. I instructed Jiff to wear a white button-down shirt.

I put the plaid outfits I made on her and Meaux. They must have liked them, because they began barking and playing with each other and chasing each other through the house. They knew they were going somewhere special.

Jiff said, "Ready? We look like a cute little family going for our Christmas pictures." I thought so too.

This pet-friendly feed store hosts monthly Yappy Hours to benefit different local rescue groups. Tonight they were hosting it for the benefit of Schnauzer Rescue, the rescue where I volunteered and managed. This was always fun for schnauzer lovers and their dogs. We arrived soon after the start time so we walked right up for the photo. There was a big red sleigh we could all fit in. Santa had to stand this one out because we filled up the sleigh, but I really didn't want some guy I didn't know sitting in the photo with all of us. Besides, even though he was wearing a Santa suit, he had black eyebrows showing and that just didn't look right. Our first Christmas photo of Jiff and me together with Meaux and Isabella turned out great. It was fitting since schnauzers are what brought us together, sort of. The lady taking the photos printed one off for us and gave us the rest on a thumb drive, all for ten dollars.

After our holiday photo, we found glasses of wine being served for us near the cheese table. I would sneak a piece of cheese to Meaux and Isabella now and then when no one was looking. Ned and Janice arrived with Kringle, who was wearing a doggie holiday sweater. When Jiff and Ned went off to get wine refills for us, Janice spilled the beans on Julia.

"I was shocked to see Patrick and Sheila at that party last night. Patrick is still having an affair with Julia right under Sheila's nose after he swore to her it was over. Sheila forgave him, but if she finds out he's back to his old tricks, I wonder how she will handle him this time. Can you believe the audacity?" Janice asked.

"Are you sure Julia's still seeing him? Frank told me she was seeing a married man. He didn't tell me who it was, only that the wife was in her gourmet cooking club. Frank thought it was over after the wife found out and confronted Julia at a class meeting in Julia's kitchen. I can't imagine why either of them would want to come to Julia's party after all that."

"Sheila is in my church group, and Julia is too. I can't imagine why Julia stays in our group or why no one has asked her to leave," Janice said.

"Are you sure Julia and Patrick are still seeing each other?" I asked her.

"Sheila and Patrick both come from influential families uptown who will make sure that marriage stays together. Sheila was working hard to forgive Patrick, but I know Patrick is still seeing Julia. I have a clear view from my kitchen window of both entrances. I can see who comes and goes out of Julia's building, both the front and the back. The back is closer and I can see it better," Janice said. "Since Sheila found out and confronted him, Patrick stopped for about a week. Now, Patrick has been going in and out Julia's back door."

"Frank told me she was seeing him until the wife found out. I don't think Frank would have told me that if it was still going on," I said. *I thought, something slipped by Frank?* "Frank is a strange guy. Frank and Julia have a weird and strange relationship, so he isn't afraid to tell her when she is doing something she shouldn't be doing. Hard to believe he is the voice of reason over there." *There was weird and strange again.*

"I see Frank leave out the front door on an errand, and then Patrick comes over within minutes. He parks in that shed she has behind the house. If Frank comes home, he goes out the back door and into the shed. She installed an automatic garage door on it. Patrick must have one of the devices to open and close it."

"I wonder why she is still seeing him when she has the new boyfriend," I mused out loud.

"Julia is using LB like she uses Ned and Frank," Janice said.

"What do you mean?"

"The day before the party, I saw LB walking around the front yard telling the workmen who delivered one of those PODs which contained all that stuff she has on display where to set it all up. She wasn't out there, he was. Then she had him pruning her bushes on the side of the house."

"Pruning her bushes?" I asked. "This isn't the time of year to prune bushes, is it?"

"I only know to prune rose bushes in winter, but I don't know what she had him cutting," she shook her head and shrugged her shoulders. "It's the one right under the third window from the front of her house on the south side—the side I can see from my kitchen window. It's the only bush I saw him cutting."

Ned and Jiff returned with our refilled wine glasses. Janice and I began to notice and comment on all the dogs dressed in holiday wear. One family came in matching pajama outfits on the parents, the two kids, and the dog. Some owners wore their holiday party clothes and their pets had a festive sweater or scarf to coordinate. There were some owners who were all about their dog's outfits and not their own. One pair of pugs wore Santa and Mrs. Claus costumes. There was a variety of elf outfits and holiday wear on big dogs, little dogs, and all sized dogs in between.

"Do you know for a fact if Frank is living at the bed and breakfast full time?" I asked Janice. "I've been meaning to ask him."

"Ned might know. Julia is always asking him to do favors for her. She asks him to help Frank move this or that. She has enough men going in and out of there. She doesn't need Ned's help," she said.

"Oh, I don't mind," Ned said. I saw Jiff raise his eyes when neither of them were looking. *I thought, Ned doesn't know when to keep his mouth shut.*

"I'm pretty sure Frank is living there," Ned said to me. "She has a double parlor upstairs in the front of the house set up for a bedroom and office with double doors that close. I think Frank sleeps on the hide-a-bed in the office. I helped him move it in there. I think he and Julia share a closet."

"That is the only thing I can't believe," I said. "Julia sharing a closet with anyone."

Ned said, "He looks like he wears her makeup."

"Ned!" Janice snapped.

"He wears somebody's makeup," Jiff said, and we all laughed. Jiff could put anyone at ease in any situation. He had the gift. When we were together, everyone we met seemed to like him. He was an agreeable guy, and I'm sure it came in very handy in court when it was important for the jury to like you and your client.

Ned asked, "So what kinda name is Jiff? Is it a nickname?"

Janice rolled her eyes and to me said, "It's the wine talking."

Jiff, with his ever-so-gracious self went on to explain how he's named after his dad, Geoffrey, but when he was a little boy they called him Geoff. Jiff used to say his name was Jiff, like the peanut butter since it sounded the same to him. The nickname stuck. Jiff and Ned started talking about football, the Saints, and who was likely to win the playoffs. While they were occupied, Janice said, "Julia is always asking favors of us. She asks me to watch her dogs, let them out, pick up her packages or newspapers, but she's always too busy to reciprocate. I have only asked one favor of her, and it was to come over and let Kringle out when I had to take Ned to the hospital for emergency gall bladder surgery. We had to leave at 3:00 a.m. When I called, she didn't answer, not that I expected her to at three in the morning. I left a message saying I was leaving our key in her mailbox, and she never called back. Frank called me and asked how Ned was doing and said he had gone over to take care of Kringle. He gave me back my key. To this day she has never asked about Ned, or even gone out of her way to make up a reason for not getting back to me."

When it looked like I was going to say something, Janice went on, "I know what you are going to ask; did Frank erase the message? I asked him that question and he said that she told him to erase it. He said 'That's how she is.'"

"Let me ask you one more thing about the day of the party. Did you see anyone leave a box about so big," I made a size with my hands, roughly the size of the box the rats came in, "at Julia's front door?" I asked. "I was there at about one-thirty in the afternoon and Frank said it had just arrived. We are wondering who sent it. There was no return address."

"The day of? No. I don't remember seeing anyone leave a package, but there were workmen there all day setting up all that crap-o-la on her front lawn," Janice said. "Why? Did someone actually send her a gift and she wants to write a thank you?"

"No, not hardly," I said. Someone waved at Janice from across the room to come get in line with them. I welcomed the distraction.

I noticed a few people who had adopted from me standing on the other side of the room, waiting to have their photos taken. Ned and Janice got in line with Kringle to take a photo. Jiff and I walked over to say hello to those who had adopted a rescued schnauzer from me and to ask how everyone was doing. After catching up and wishing my extended schnauzer family a Yappy Holiday, I spotted Hanky with her dog Valentine with Detective Taylor. They had moved into Ned and Janice's place near the cheese table.

Hanky and Taylor were drinking bottles of water from the big ice bucket on the cheese table. "Mr. GQ and I are technically still on duty," Hanky said. Taylor acted like he didn't hear her. "I wanted to get my photo taken with Valentine or just one of him, but that line is too long. We only have thirty minutes left on our dinner break before we have to get back. I forgot his search and rescue ID badge too. Oh well."

"Come on. I know almost everyone in line and I'll get you to the front of it," I said. Then I looked at Taylor and said, "Give me your shield."

"What?" he asked me and looked like I just asked him to shoot someone.

"Give me your shield. For this to work, Valentine has to be an NOPD canine on dinner break," I said, holding out my hand.

Jiff and Hanky nodded to him in the direction of my hand. Painfully slow, he handed over his shield saying, "Are you guys for real?"

Jiff told him, "It's her world; I'm just in it."

"Hanky, I'll put yours on Valentine's collar in case someone gets close enough to read the name. You hold Taylor's," I said.

We walked up to the front of the line and I asked out loud, "May I have everyone's attention?" When they all stopped talking and looked at me, I said, "This detective adopted this little schnauzer from me after he helped find a missing person buried in a backyard." *I left off the fact that Valentine and Meaux dug up the body in my backyard while I was fostering him.* "Now he's a working dog. They are on their dinner break and only have thirty minutes before they are due back at work. Does anyone mind if Detective Hanky and her dog get their photo taken ahead of you? They are working a homicide."

"No, no, go ahead," most people said. One or two looked a little put off and grumpy, but the overwhelming sense of good cheer squashed any complaints.

Technically, Valentine did work for the NOPD once, and now he's a volunteer with Hanky when she goes to storm or tornado-damaged areas on her time off to aid in recovery efforts. Hanky thought he was a great little dog and fell in love with him the second he jumped in her lap and kissed her face, even before she knew he would make a great search and rescue dog. Valentine is a natural and finds people in collapsed structures or people who have been missing.

We waited while a lady dressed like Mrs. Claus and a female Weimaraner dressed like a Raggedy Ann got in position for their photo. The big dog had a red wig with pigtails and when she sat down, the dog's front legs were the doll legs and the top of the dress had arms off the shoulders so she looked like Raggedy Ann standing up. Her other dog was small, a rat terrier dressed like a clown. She had a large-size jack-in-the-box with the rear panel cut out, so when she placed it on the floor, the little dog ran into it from behind and put his head up through the top to look like he "popped" out of the box.

After Hanky and Valentine were snapped, we went back to Jiff and Taylor.

"People make a big production here out of dog pictures with Santa," Taylor said, looking at one man walk by to take a photo in his tux with tails and top hat, while his white Great Dane also wore a tuxedo with tails and a top hat. The Dane looked like he wore a rental that would fit a small person, maybe a child or Frank.

Jiff said, "This is nothing. Wait until you see Barkus. Barkus is the Mardi Gras parade just for dogs. Hundreds of people with their pets show up in costumes—very elaborate costumes."

"People make floats for their pets. There's marching dog bands…you have to see it," I said.

Hanky leaned into Taylor and said, "Let's not make a production of exchanging shields in here. We might get Brandy run out of her own party." Taylor nodded and Hanky said, "Wait until we get in the car." To me, she said, "Thanks, Brandy. That line is going to take an hour or more to get through. I hope it makes good money for your rescue group."

"Yeah, it looks long and more people are coming in now," I said nodding at the door.

"You do rescue?" Taylor asked. "For dogs?"

"For schnauzers only. She is a breed specific rescue," Jiff answered. "That's how we met."

"Is that your day job?" Taylor asked.

"Hardly. I work for a telecom company in fraud prevention," I said. "I try to find bad guys hacking companies to rip them off. You guys have a gun. I have a computer print out."

Hanky said, "Don't let that face fool you, Taylor. She sees patterns where some of us don't. She helped us with a case not too long ago." She looked at her watch and said they had to get back to work. I walked with them to the door while Jiff held both dogs on their leashes. "Janice and Ned from the party last night were just here. I think they're still in line. She just told me something interesting. It could be important. Pick me up tomorrow so we can drive together and I'll update you."

"Okay, and thanks for your help with the photo," Hanky said, getting in the squad car. Valentine sat in the front between them.

Jiff and I stayed a bit longer so I could visit with some of my adoptive schnauzer families I hadn't seen in awhile. When we did head home, it was with two very tired paw-ty animals and more dirt on Julia than I really wanted to know.

Chapter Ten

AFTER I FED Meaux, I called the president of the cooking club, Ms. Agnes Reyes. Frank said she was elderly and probably couldn't hear well. If that turned out to be the case, then I'd ask, loudly, if I could come visit her.

"Ms. Reyes," I said after hearing a soft-spoken hello on the other end of the call.

"Yes. This is Agnes Reyes. Who is this?"

After I introduced myself and stated the reason for the call, Ms. Reyes asked me to call her Agnes. I was speaking in a normal voice—not a raised voice—that she could hear perfectly fine.

"Can you tell me whose names were assigned the numbers for the blind rum ball taste exchange?" I asked after I explained Julia's brother had been eating a box when he appeared to have been poisoned.

"Certainly. Let me get my notebook for the club." She left the phone for a moment and returned saying, "Okay, is there a number in particular, or do you want all eight of them?"

I asked for all eight and wrote them down as she dictated the names and numbers. She went on to say that her number had been number eight and confirmed Julia was number three. She went on to explain that she ordered the boxes so they would all be uniform to make the exchange more fun and in keeping with the blind taste test.

I asked Agnes if she sent her box with toothpicks of any sort or knew of anyone in the club who liked to use flowers or parts of plants for garnish. She said she didn't send anything in her box except rum balls. She checked all the boxes and numbered them before she had her grandson drop them at Julia's. She made sure only rum balls would be in the boxes and the members couldn't give any clues as to which box was theirs to influence voting.

"Could someone have hidden a clue on the bottom, inside the box?" I asked.

"Maybe, but I looked in every box and I think I would have seen something there other than rum balls," Agnes said.

"Thanks for your time and for speaking with me," I said.

"That is terrible for that young man and his new wife," Agnes said. "I know some of the members don't like Julia, but I truly do not think someone in our club would go to that extreme. She can be a tad bit much to take from time to time. I've known all of these women, and their mothers, since they were little girls. I started this cooking club with their grandmothers."

"Yes, I agree. I've known Julia a while, and she often speaks first without thinking," I said.

"And she speaks rather loudly. You should talk to her about that," Agnes said. "She might need to have her hearing checked."

I imagined seeing a smile on the face of the lady at the other end of the call.

I thanked her and hung up. Agnes was sharp and seemed on top of the goings on with the cooking club. I hoped her eyesight was as good when she checked every box.

HANKY ARRIVED A few minutes before one o'clock and honked the horn for me to come out. I walked outside and was about to open the back door to get in the squad car when Detective Taylor leaned out of his window and said, "You really don't want to sit in the back. We won't even put Valentine back there. You might want to follow us in your vehicle."

"Right," I said. "Well, let me tell you this before we get there. Frank knows a lot more of what goes on over there than even Julia suspects. He told me Julia was having an affair with the husband of one couple who showed up at the party. The wife is in Julia's Pilates class and gourmet cooking club. She found out and confronted Julia and thought the affair ended. I think Frank did too. The neighbors who live across the street, the ones you saw at the Yappy Hour last night, told me Julia is still seeing him."

"This just keeps getting better," Hanky said.

"I think there's more than just that. You need to get Frank talking and not let him think you see him as a suspect. Otherwise, he will start crying if he feels threatened, and you won't get any useful information from him," I said.

"Crying?" Detective Taylor asked and had an exasperated look of disbelief on his face.

"They are a different sort of couple," Hanky said.

"Well, I wouldn't call them a couple," I said. "I see them more along the lines like those symbiotic pairings. You know, like a shark and remora, or the bird that sits in the alligator's mouth, trusting the alligator not to eat it?"

"Well, we all know which one Julia is," Hanky said.

"I have to be home by five o'clock at the latest. Jiff and I have plans to go caroling in Jackson Square."

"You're going caroling? Aren't you afraid someone will release a pack of barking dogs on you and try to run you off?" Taylor asked with just a hint of a smile.

🍸 🍸 🍸

WE WERE ALL in Julia's double parlor opposite the dining room where Larry's body and Donna had been found. There was still crime scene tape across the dining room doors. Hanky and Taylor were standing while the rest of us were seated.

"I asked Brandy to come here because she knows you both and might be able to contribute to something one or more of you saw the night all this happened," Hanky said.

I asked, "Frank, what did you do with that gold foil box that looked like all the other rum ball boxes Jiff and I gave to you last night?" By way of explanation to the confused look on Julia's and Hanky's faces I added, "Jiff and I saw something in the mailbox the night we arrived so we brought it in." I didn't want to be the tell-all on Julia with the unhappy neighbor over the lights, Pilates, gourmet cooking group, neighborhood association, and the rats in the box. We would get to that soon enough.

"Oh, right, that box. I left it outside on the back porch. Well, not outside, but I hid it in the dryer so no one would find it," he said. Then he jumped up and ran off in the direction of the porch.

"There's another box of rum balls?" Hanky asked.

"Why…" both Julia and Hanky started to ask.

"Why did we give it to Frank?" I finished for them. "I'll let him give you the details on some of the stuff he told me Friday morning. The box had a note on it about…you'll see when Frank brings it back." I asked Hanky, "Did your forensics group have anything unusual on or in the rum ball boxes they took to examine?"

"I'm waiting on a call with those results," Hanky said.

"I'll check while we wait on Frank," Detective Taylor offered. He walked into the hall to make his call.

Frank came in with a gold box identical to the two rum ball boxes that Larry had been eating from. I nodded toward Hanky for him to hand it to her. She had a plastic evidence bag she opened so Frank could drop the gold foil box into it.

"Yes, it looks like the same box with the note Jiff and I brought in. Julia, you said all of your gourmet cooking club made rum balls, but only the president knew who made which box because they were numbered? Isn't that right?"

Julia nodded yes. Detective Taylor came back into the room.

"This box doesn't have a number." I nodded toward it, and Hanky handed the plastic bag with the gold foil box in it to Taylor.

"We'll take it and have them analyze what's in it, and maybe we can get prints from the boxes to see who handled which one besides Frank," Hanky said. "This box might be contaminated, but no one ate anything from it. We still need to confirm if it's a group effort that caused the death of your brother or if it's one misdirected individual."

"Frank, tell Detective Hanky the other stuff you told me yesterday. You know, the box that was left anonymously on the front step, the person who complained about the two deer and left the signed note—everything you remember." I said. "Tell them about the rats."

Frank started crying.

"What rats?" Julia asked as she handed him a tissue from the box she had been carrying around under her arm. Her eyes were red from crying, so she was slow on the uptake. "Rats? Here?"

"Before he answers," I said turning to Julia, "have you had any arguments with your pest control people?"

"No. Why are you asking me that?" Julia snapped.

"Brandy stood by you when you were arrested for murder when everyone else thought you were guilty, including me," Hanky said. "It's to your advantage to have her here, but if you want her gone…" Hanky's stinging comments seemed to shame Julia into realizing she might be in the hot seat. Julia shrugged by way of answering.

"Frank," Hanky tapped her notepad. "Rats."

Frank said he didn't want to scare or worry Julia with everything else going on, and she was planning a nice party. Frank gave a very complete accounting about the rats in the box and why he asked me to open it, what was written on the bottom, the note from The Christian neighbor, and the warning from the Neighborhood Business Association. It was much the same as he told me, and I didn't hear anything new or remember something he may have forgotten. Julia was horrified at the rats in the box and had no idea who could have done it.

"Tell us who didn't come to the party and why they might have wanted to harm you or why they don't like you," Hanky said.

I gave Frank a look to keep quiet.

Julia gave Hanky the names of several neighbors who didn't respond to the party invitation. She thought some of them might have less than a warm-and-fuzzy feeling toward her.

"Let's see," Hanky started to recap. "The Neighborhood Association voted to fine you; one neighbor left an unsigned note saying he or she was Christian, implying you are not; another anonymous sender left you three rats in a box; and the Secret Santas from the gourmet cooking club all gave you rum balls that might be poisoned. Did I leave anything out?"

Frank raised his hand to speak. I guess the look I gave him was more effective than I intended. "What else can you add, Frank?" Hanky asked.

He looked at Julia before he started to speak. "There's also the neighbor's two high school boys Julia called the cops on."

"What was the complaint?" Detective Taylor asked.

"It was when she first put the reindeer on the front lawn. She saw two neighbor boys messing around with them and told them to get off her lawn."

Detective Taylor was making notes and asked Frank, "Did these boys destroy property?" He also would sneak a peek at Julia, checking out her reactions when Frank's story was unfolding.

"Wait a minute," Julia started to say, and Hanky shushed her, holding up a hand like she was stopping traffic.

"Frank, what else?" Hanky asked.

"Well, we're not sure it was them. It most likely was them because the next morning the deer were arranged to make it look like they were mating. The parents begged Julia not to press charges for fear it would ruin their chances at the Ivy League school the boys were being considered for," Frank finished and would not return Julia's stare.

Detective Taylor asked Julia, "Miss Richard, what did these boys do to provoke you to call in a complaint?"

Julia pounced on the first silent second to go into her rant, "My neighbors spawned monsters and refer to them as their children. One is always being arrested for one thing or another. I see their names and addresses in the paper every other day," Julia stated as if this was common knowledge.

"When she sees one mentioned in the newspaper, she goes looking for the parents when she's walking the dogs so she can rub it in that their kid was the one arrested," Frank said while doing a heavy eye roll. "Most of the neighbors don't like her."

"So, let's add all neighbors with children to the list that might want to see you dead, or who'd want to poison you, right?" Hanky finished and closed her notebook. "Is there anyone you haven't offended, because I don't want to go door to door questioning people if they didn't come to the party or might be someone you haven't had an issue with. That might remind them of a reason they should have a grudge. We don't need to look for more suspects. I have enough here to keep this investigation going for months."

"Miss Richard, who came to this party and knew your brother and his new wife?" Detective Taylor asked.

Julia sat up a little straighter and tossed her hair when Detective Taylor spoke to her. "No one else knew them, but several people knew of them," she answered.

"What do you mean? Knew of them?" Taylor asked.

"I've talked about my brother… all right. I complained about my brother—you know family stuff—to Brandy and Frank," Julia said. "No one at the party knew him or ever met him before."

"What about your brother's new wife? Did anybody here know her before last night or know her from some place else?" Detective Taylor asked.

"I have no idea. I only met her yesterday at four o'clock in the afternoon before the party. They got here three hours early, so I asked them to go spend a couple of hours in the French Quarter so I could finish the party preparations," Julia answered.

"What about your neighbors across the street?" Hanky asked. "Did they know your brother and his new wife?"

"No, I really don't talk to them much and I don't socialize with them," Julia answered.

I saw Frank do an eye roll.

Hanky then asked, "Julia, this man you've been seeing, how well do you know him?"

Julia started to answer she met LB at a bar and Hanky interrupted her. "No, not LB, Patrick MacFinn. Sheila MacFinn's husband. How did that start and how long have you been having an affair with him?"

All the color drained from Julia's face. First the rats and now this. Julia didn't like being caught off guard.

"Did Sheila tell you that? We ended it when Sheila found out, and we all decided to remain friends." Julia turned slightly in her chair away from Hanky and folded her arms and crossed her legs.

Hanky looked at Frank. I felt sorry for him because he looked pitiful and about to cry. "What do you know about Miss Richard's affair with Patrick MacFinn? Did you ever see them together?"

"All right, I'll tell you," Julia snapped. "Don't drag him into this. Sheila is in my Pilates class and her husband offered me a ride home one evening when he came to pick up Sheila, but she didn't make that class. I invited him in for a glass of wine, and well, you know…" Julia answered sharply.

"How long ago was this? The glass of wine and …you know…?" asked Detective Taylor.

Julia's face was reddening and her jaw was set. I didn't think she was going to answer, but then she said, "Six weeks ago. It started six weeks ago."

"How did his wife find out?" Detective Taylor asked.

"He must have told her," Julia said.

"No man on this planet would volunteer that information to his wife, so how do you think she found out?" Taylor asked again.

"One of the busybody ladies in my gourmet cooking club who is also in my Pilates class must have told her. Possibly Bicky, Bicky Favalara. She saw him give me a ride home that day and two more times after that when Sheila didn't come to class or went to another one," Julia said.

Detective Taylor looked at Julia and said, "And?"

"Patrick thinks Bicky might have followed us or she saw him leaving my house later that afternoon and told his wife. I guess Sheila put it together or she asked him when he got home," Julia answered.

"So, how did it come about they were here for your party?" Hanky asked. "Seems odd if you were having an affair with her husband, and she knew it, that she would agree to come to a party at your house."

"I apologized to Sheila, and she was good with that, so we all moved on," Julia pulled out another tissue from the box under her arm.

"When did she find out?" Detective Taylor asked.

"I don't remember exactly," Julia said.

"About a week before the party," Frank answered. "They were all here in the kitchen for a class. Sheila threw a handful of flour at Julia in front of all the members and then tossed the rest of the bag all over everything in the kitchen."

"So, a week ago, a woman finds out you are having an affair with her husband, flours you, then finds it in her heart to forgive you both and comes to your home for a Christmas party?" Taylor asked. "She either has an attorney filing to divorce him for everything he has, or she wants to harm, maybe only embarrass you. I don't think her marriage and your friendship moved on to Nirvana in only a week."

"Bicky Favalara? Is she related to Favalara Pest Control?" I asked. "The slogans on their trucks say they are Termite-NATORS, E-Rat-OCATERS and D-Bug-GERS. Not very original but memorable."

"Bicky and her husband own it," Julia said. "Bicky is married to Sheila's brother. I remember them talking about that at a Pilates meeting."

"Bicky told Sheila you left Pilates with her husband?" I asked Julia. "I think we can guess where the rats came from."

Hanky said, "We'll follow up with Mr. Favalara and ask how he e-Rat-ocates his rodents or where he sends them.

Where can we find your boyfriend? Now I'm talking about the person you refer to as LB. Do you have a phone number to reach him?"

Julia gave Hanky an 800 number. "He uses that for his business associates to contact him on. It's a free call. That's the only number I have."

"What's his full name?" Hanky asked.

"LB Sutton. I don't know what the LB stands for," Julia said.

I made a mental note of the 800 number in case I had to find him or Julia with him.

Chapter Eleven

ANKY AND TAYLOR left saying they would be back once they went to the lab and talked with the coroner to see what actually killed Larry Richard. I stayed to tell Julia if she didn't want me here I understood.

"No, she needs you here," Frank said to me before she could answer. "Julia, tell her who called right before you got here."

"Frank, you're going to find yourself without a job when this is all over if you don't quit blurting things out," Julia said and turned to me. "Larry's boss called me. I gave the hospital the name of the company where Larry worked so they could verify Donna was on his medical insurance. The hospital also informed Larry's boss that he had died. I guess Larry had me listed as his next of kin and hadn't updated it with Donna's information."

"What do they need you to do?" I asked.

"They want me to go to their office in Houma to sign some papers and get his belongings from his desk and locker. Donna won't be out of the hospital for a few more days," Julia said. "They said it's my name on the paperwork, and I need to go there to sign it in front of their attorney and pick up his things."

"I'll go with you if you want me to, but wouldn't you rather have LB go with you?" I asked.

"Donna is getting released tomorrow, and LB said he'd pick her up and bring her here. I said she could stay here a couple of days before she decides what to do or go home," Julia said.

"Well, there's the matter of the funeral. I think she might want to be here or help with that," I said as gently as I could.

"I'd just as soon tell the hospital to send him someplace to be cremated. I don't want to go back to the hospital or talk to Donna about any of this. Let LB deal with her helpless, brainless questions she'll start asking as soon as she's released," Julia said.

"Julia, you need to keep thoughts like that in here," I said tapping my head. "Try not to let them out here." I made a motion with my hands as if pulling something out of my mouth in front of me.

Frank added, "Do you know how insulting you sound when you make comments like that?"

"I don't care if people get their panties in a wad over every little thing I say," she huffed.

"Did you tell one of the church ladies, who offered to bring something to your party, to keep her Tupperware home because you didn't want chips and dip served here, or pigs-in-a-blanket?" I asked.

"I didn't want my party turning into a potluck dinner. That's what every get-together looks like anytime you have women bringing a dish. It always looks like whatever they made is baked and burned all over their harvest pattern Corning Ware," she said. "I wanted my dinner to look nice and for everything to have a pretty presentation."

"Even when you say it, she doesn't hear how it sounds," Frank said to me.

"Frank, I'm warning you. You are dancing on my last nerve," she said and slapped her hand on the arm of her chair.

"Look, just think how can you make what you want to say sound like a compliment. You could have told them you appreciate the offer but not to go to any trouble because you have planned out the dinner and all the side dishes and already have too much food. If they like bringing a dish, you will ask them to next time, okay?"

"Half of them would bring it anyway," Julia huffed.

"Well, put it in the kitchen, and when they're not looking, empty it into one of your serving dishes.

"Julia, I hope you know Frank and I are both here out of concern for you," I said. "If you don't need me…"

"Will you go with me tomorrow?" Julia asked me. "Frank can stay here and help LB with Donna."

On my way home, I drove past three of the homes where members of the cooking club lived who turned in a box of rum balls for the exchange. I had looked up their addresses once Agnes gave me their names. I didn't know what I was looking for, but I sure hoped I'd know it when I saw it. I planned to drive by all of the other seven members' homes. Every member's yard had blankets or sheets over the shrubbery to protect them from freezing temperatures that had been forecasted for the past week and predicted to continue for the next few days until after Christmas.

I PICKED JULIA up at 7:00 a.m., and we headed west toward Houma. I drove because I had a customer I had done several network repairs and reviews for in Raceland but had never met. Everything was done over the phone and via computer, voice mail, emails, and texts. Sooner or later he was going to call again with an issue. He needed an overall system upgrade, replacing a lot of outdated software. I decided I'd pop in on my way home and tell him how nice it was working with him, and since I was in the neighborhood, I wanted to meet him. We'd pass right by his pipe manufacturing business on our way back to New Orleans, and it was always easier to tell someone how much the fix would cost after you met him face-to-face. At least, it seemed that way to me.

We took the 310 split out of Kenner to the Highway 90 exit. Then it was a divided highway for the remainder of the trip with stoplights, crossovers, and speed traps in varying speed zones. Highway 90, in this part of the state, looks like an endless collection of metal prefab buildings in between boarded-up, single-story commercial spaces. Buildings that weren't boarded either had a sign that said, "Bar," "Restaurant," "Restaurant & Bar," or a neon sign that just said "OPEN." You had to guess if it was a bar, a restaurant, or a bar *and a* restaurant. This strip of highway reminded me of how Julia described the places Larry liked to frequent…honky tonks.

"Larry might have frequented some of these restaurants along here, don't you think?" I asked her, trying to get her talking.

"Hmm. Maybe," Julia said, staring out the window as I drove.

The only redeeming quality of every one of these places was the food. These Cajun boys know how to cook. Kitchens in this part of the state are mobile, set up on a wire bed trailer that could be hooked up to a trailer hitch should the chef be summoned elsewhere to prepare food for an event. These mobile outdoor kitchens, some more tricked out than others, produced the most delicately fried fish or seafood, perfectly spiced boiled crawfish or shrimp, and big mouth-watering pots of gumbo. They were equipped with nothing more than propane tanks, big sixty-gallon boiling pots, big frying pans, and all the beer the chef needed to turn out enough food for a Cajun festival. The most fascinating thing about watching these guys cook was the outfits they wore and their custom-made utensils.

The dress code called for everyone to wear white or black shrimp boots. Cajun cooks fashioned a big utensil out of something handy. One guy used a boat oar and another used a broomstick with a colander wired to the end to stir or scoop out mudbugs to see if they were done!

It took us an hour and a half to drive to the headquarter location for the Houma, Morgan City, and Thibodeaux branch of the company Larry worked for. When we parked the car at our destination, I noticed this building was shiny and freshly painted, with landscaping and a sprinkler system. I expected as much. The oil industry was the big kahuna around here. Almost everyone in southwest Louisiana from Houma to Lake Charles was either employed by the oil industry, worked to feed those employed by the oil industry, or taught the children of those employed by the oil industry.

Julia had been quiet for most of the ride. I figured she'd loosen up after we both met with the company people and were told what they wanted from her. I used the time to call a few clients and wish them a nice holiday.

Before we got out of the car, Julia asked me, "Do you think I should tell them Larry was married?"

"I think we should go in here and be honest. Let's see what they want to tell you, give you, or ask you for," I said and looked at her. Julia sat there staring at the back of the truck parked in front of us. "What is it? Something bothering you?" I thought maybe Larry's death was just hitting her.

"You see that truck with the airbrushed wolf on the back window?"

"Yes," I said.

"I should have driven Larry's pickup truck here with a FOR SALE sign on it. I bet I could've sold it in five minutes. It's got that same tacky wolf painted on his back window to hide his gun rack."

"Worry about that later," I said. "Let's go."

A pretty young girl greeted us and said, "Oh yes, Miz Richard, they are expecting you. Right this way, cher."

Everybody down here called each other cher. It was an endearment like calling someone honey.

The walls throughout the waiting room, the corridor we walked down to get to the meeting, and the conference room were covered with giant photos of oil rigs and platforms. The photos on desks were of loved ones in hard hats, safety vests, blue jeans, and work boots. We passed several cubicles where two or three men sat talking in the local dialect, Cajun French. I know a little French from high school, but I couldn't make out a word they said. The sound of their language has its own lilt and did not resemble true French at all. It was pretty, relaxed, and pleasant to hear. I'd love to learn it.

She led us to meet with three men waiting in a glass-walled conference room with comfortable swivel chairs, a whiteboard on one end, and a recessed screen for power point presentations on the other. All the AV equipment looked state of the art. We all introduced ourselves. Mr. Babineaux offered us coffee, water, or any other drink we'd like. Julia and I accepted coffee. The girl who accompanied us to the conference room was dispatched to get our preferences. Mr. Authement advised us he was the attorney for the company and gave his condolences to Julia on behalf of the men there and the company.

"Larry Richard, your brother, was a good worker and never missed a day. He was liked by his fellow workers and well-thought-of by management. We are sorry to hear he has left us in this untimely manner," Mr. Authement said. "Our condolences to you and your family, Miss Richard."

"Thank you," Julia said, barely audible. "I'm the only family left. My brother got married two weeks ago, and the woman he married is still in the hospital from something. We don't even know yet. Did Larry add her to his health insurance?"

"Yes, he did, but it takes ninety days for it to go into effect, I'm sorry to say," Mr. Babineaux answered. "I'm the human resources director. Mr. Chiasson is the sales and marketing manager over the division your brother worked for."

Mr. Chiasson said, "Larry had a few months in accrued vacation owed him. He rarely took a day off. He worked all the time. We wanted to give you his back pay and his life insurance claim. Ms. Richard, Larry named you as his beneficiary."

Julia and I were both stunned and looked at each other for an explanation.

"We know he got married, and he came in to add his wife to his medical plan, but he did not want to make changes to any other benefits," Mr. Chiasson said and looked at both of us. "I asked Larry if he wanted to change anything else and he said no. He wanted to leave everything to you." He handed Julia two checks. The one for the vacation pay was in the amount of thirty thousand dollars, and the life insurance payout was one hundred fifty thousand.

Mr. Authement went on to add, "We know families can use the money right away for funeral expenses to help make the arrangements. Here, we try to get the help to the insured's family right away."

This wasn't the picture of Larry we were expecting. They asked Julia to sign for receipt of the checks and she did. This wasn't a job-related accident so it was nice they wanted to help families get money sooner rather than later. I'm sure this was a much less stressful way to lose an employee instead of by accident on a rig.

"Come eat with us," Mr. Babineaux said. "We're having our Christmas lunch here at headquarters. We have a big, nice lunch every day this week while the men are doing a shift change. The ones going out come here before they leave, and the ones coming in off the rigs stop to get their bonus checks and have a bite with their fellow workers. We all sit and eat together. Larry knew almost all of these guys from the rigs. He sold them equipment they needed and then he'd go out and make sure there were no problems with it. He was a good troubleshooter."

Before Julia could say something insulting, I said, "That's a great idea, and we would love to. Is there a ladies' room where we can freshen up?" They pointed down the hall to the left. I practically dragged her with me.

"I don't want to eat here," Julia said as soon as we were in the bathroom.

"Let's keep anything you want to say in here," I tapped my head. "Let's not let it come out here," and I put my finger over my mouth. "They just handed you almost two hundred thousand dollars. These people are nice and have invited us, so yes, we, and by we, I mean you are having lunch here," I said as I reapplied my lipstick. Julia had already fluffed her hair and was pulling out a compact to reapply more face powder she didn't need. "We're here and you might learn something else about your brother. You won't get any better chances than this."

"I know all I need to know..." Julia said.

"Really? Did you expect him to leave you that money? He could have changed that when he married Donna. I think you need to act a little grateful and try to see your brother like these people knew him. He seems like he tried to do the right thing by you, his only family left."

Julia looked at me unconvinced. "You did meet Twilight with the black eye, right?"

I said, "I never heard Twilight or your brother say she got that from him. Do you really know if he was the one who hit her?"

"You don't know him. He's just like my daddy was, fast with his hands," Julia said.

"Too bad he had such a bad role model. You got away from your dad and saw how things should be. Maybe after your dad died, Larry saw things differently," I said. Julia still didn't look convinced. "When we get back I think you should ask Donna and get all the facts before you make up your mind about your only brother."

"We'll see when we get back," Julia said. "I still don't want to eat here."

"You can eat here with me or sit in the car and freeze while while I accept their invitation and have lunch. Your choice." I said, "I won't even give you the keys to turn on the heat while you wait."

Julia stared at me.

"It could get a little chilly out there," I said as I started to leave the ladies' room.

"Okay," she said.

"Julia, be nice or I will leave you out on the highway and you can walk home," I said.

With her luck she would meet a wealthy oil man to give her a ride.

Chapter Twelve

M R. CHAISSON MET us in the hallway and took us to a large room that spread across the entire width of the building. It looked like it could be used for meetings since there was a stage at one end and a cafeteria-style kitchen at the other. Today, it sat at least one hundred people—picnic style—at lunch tables with benches. Julia was going to love this.

He announced and introduced us as Larry Richard's sister and her friend. He said we had graciously accepted their offer to eat with them. Okay, so most of it was right.

All stood and the ones wearing baseball caps tapped them while everyone mumbled condolences.

Mr. Chaisson led us over to a table and said, "Sit here by Andre and T-Jean. They knew Larry very well and worked with him a lot over the years. I'll be back to join you."

All the men up and down the picnic-style table stood up as we were brought over. Andre said, "We all install what Larry sells, but Larry, he makes it work if there are problems, cher."

"I'm Brandy and this is Larry's sister Julia," I said by way of introduction.

"I'm Andre and this is T-Jean," he said and pointed across the room. "His dad is over there. We call him Poppa Jean or just Pop. They both answer to almost anything when it's time to eat." All the men at the table laughed. T-Jean gave Andre a good-natured push.

Cajuns call little John or John Jr. petit John, but just say the "T" before the name. His dad was Jean.

"T-Jean's mamma is making crawfish étouffée today. We'll get you a plate," Andre said as he and T-Jean made a beeline for the food.

"Not too much," Julia and I said at the same time, but no one heard us.

Andre and T-Jean came back with two trays and man-size meals that would satisfy a lumberjack or in this case, a roughneck off the rigs.

"Eat what you want," T-Jean said. "My Mamma can box it up and you take home what you don't eat, unless you don't like it." He looked stricken like he was afraid we would have nothing to eat if we didn't like it.

I took a bite and said, "I might not need a box for mine." Everyone smiled and dug into their meals.

"So how was my brother to work with?" Julia asked. "You guys go out and party with him too?"

Okay, I wanted to push her face into the whole plate of étouffée only it was too good to waste like that.

"Larry was single and went out a lot," Andre said between big bites of étouffée, which he helped onto his fork with a steamy piece of fresh French bread he pulled off the loaf in the basket in the middle of the table. I got a whiff of the heavenly smell from where I sat when he lifted the towel wrapped around it to keep it warm to tear a piece for himself before he passed it down the table. "We all from lil' towns out down this way. Larry, he was from our state capitol, Baton Rouge. We all figured him to be more worldly, being from the big city and all."

"Larry?" Julia asked, and I cut her off by way of a kick under the table.

"Baton Rouge is really more of a college town. It only seems like a big city because LSU is there," I said.

"Right. You ladies…you both from New Orleans?" Andre asked.

"I'm born and raised there, and Julia is from Baton Rouge but lives in New Orleans now," I answered before she could say something stupid. Then I noticed she wasn't about to talk with them, but they had the good manners to assume she was grief-stricken over Larry.

Andre, who seemed to be the self appointed spokesperson to the two of us, said, "Larry wasn't good with women. In fact, I told him, don't change everything just yet, wait till you see how it goes. I talked to him right after he stopped by and told us he got married." He went on, "Larry was always very serious at the job. Always following up, doing what he must and then some. After work, we all go home to our families, and sometimes we take him. We all married the girl we sat next to in first grade. We all got married in the same Catholic church and we all bury our relatives in the same cemetery next to that church. Your brother was not so lucky. He was lonely," Andre said.

🍸 🍸 🍸

"He always seemed to go for the one who needed the most help or looked the most lost," T-Jean said. "But, your brother loved a good party."

"We're all sorry he's missing this big party," a man sitting across from us said. "Larry, he loved the holidays, cher, and he loved when we all got together here to eat."

Another man sitting close by added, "He'd stay all afternoon talking to guys coming in off the rigs. He had a bottle of wine for each one of us to take home for our holiday dinner with our families. It's nice you're here on his behalf. We all liked Larry and we liked working with him."

"He was looking for love in all the wrong places, cher," Andre said. "We all heard about the one he married. We know her cuz she grew up around here. Her real name is not Donna Twilight or whatever it was she told Larry. Her real name is Cherie Sassone."

"Larry said he met her …" Julia started to say.

"Speed dating, he said he met her speed dating, remember, Julia? I met them both at the party the other night." I cut her off before she could say something I'd have to kick her for again. Julia nodded.

She was being very antisocial given the fact we were surrounded by all these men. At any other time, given this much male attention, Julia would have been in her element, but these were working men. They wore jeans, flannel shirts, and work boots, not business suits. Julia was a bit of a snob and too bad for her. Some of these guys worked the rigs, yes, because they either owned them, inherited them, or they were on their land and got paid based on oil production from the wells. Some of these men were likely millionaires. We were the only two women in the dining hall besides Andre's mom, and she was serving the food she cooked. The receptionist came in, got a plate, and left. I assume she went back to her position at the front door.

"Speed dating, huh?" Andre shook his head. "That poor girl had a rough life, and I think Larry just wanted to help her. He seemed to have a soft spot for ones who looked broken."

"Rough life? What do you mean?" I asked while Julia sat looking at her food and poking at it. I stepped on her foot under the table.

The three guys sitting by us looked at each other. I nodded for them to go on.

"She grew up with an alcoholic mom and a very abusive father. Her dad knocked the mom around until he killed her. Cherie ran away from home when that happened," Andre said between bites.

"We'd seen her with a black eye or two at school. Her dad went to jail, and Cherie started working in the bars at thirteen," T-Jean added. "She was a good-looking girl and with makeup she looked older, a lot older."

"Yeah, some guy outta Houston started buying up these bars where young girls worked and made them into exotic dance clubs," Andre said.

The men who were just talking about Larry all looked at their plates and took a few bites. They were too polite to call them what they were – titty bars – or call Donna—Twilight—Cherie—whatever her name really is, a stripper in front of us.

"Recently, those bars started adding speed dating," a man sitting about two seats down said. His name was Henry and the others pronounced it like the French do, On Ree.

"And how do you know all this about the bars?" Julia asked with a tinge of sarcasm.

Andre put down his fork. "Because we see the neon sign flashing in the window telling us when we pass them on our way home."

"So how many children do you each have?" I asked before Julia could say another thing.

"T-Jean has five girls," Andre said picking up his fork, grateful for the interest in his family. "I have three boys. He's gonna be working to get them girls married off for the rest of his life." That brought a round of laughter from the fellas sitting close to us.

"Who did Andre's boys sit next to in first grade?" I asked.

"His boys better not sit next to my girls," T-Jean joked.

"All my boys are gonna go to LSU and play football like I did. Of course, I'll make them get a degree for something other than engineering on an oil rig. This work has gotten too dangerous. We work hard so we can send our kids to LSU."

"And thank God we make it home when our shift is over," T-Jean added as his mother moved over to him and poured another heaping spoonful of crawfish étouffée on his plate.

T-Jean's mamma dished out seconds or thirds while asking us if we wanted bread pudding for desert. Julia and I declined.

A powerful strong smell of whiskey sauce announced Mamma's approach with the pan of bread pudding. She pulled a big ice cream scoop of pudding out of the baking pan and dropped it on our plates saying, "You both are too skinny. Cher, I bet you two have to jump around in the shower to get wet. Eat the pudding." She moved on to the guys, serving without asking.

We ate our lunch with some nice, gentlemanly comradery. Andre and T-Jean were true to their word. They boxed up what was left of our lunch and gave it to us to take home. I was stuffed and still had three-fourths of my meal left. Julia was about the same, plus we now had a big whopping serving of bread pudding for dessert. My boxed lunch felt like it weighed ten pounds.

When I got up to bring my tray to where I saw the men leaving theirs, Andre walked alongside me and said, "Follow me and I'll show you where that goes."

Once we were away from the table, Andre looked at me and said, "Look, I don't want to cause any trouble, but you two ladies seem nice. Larry got mixed up with the wrong ones trying to help Cherie. We only knew he was married to her after the fact. Cherie had a hard life and got mixed up in God only knows what. Watch out for your friend."

Andre gave Julia his card and said, "Here's my card. We'll let the other fellas know when you have the services. If we not out on the rigs, we'll be there, and please let Cherie know we are sorry for her loss."

Before Julia could start in on her plans to cremate Larry, I said, "We will let you know if there are services or a memorial. Julia's not sure what she and Donna, I mean Cherie, will plan. They have to wait on the coroner to release his body."

"Oh, right, right, right," Andre said. He put on his baseball hat that was tucked in the back of his pants, tipped it our way, and walked off.

"Sorry for your loss, Miss Julia," the men said leaving the lunch room.

Y Y Y

IN THE CAR on the way home, I said, "I'm sure this is a lot to take in. Look, I'm gonna stop up here for five minutes at a client's office. I have a bottle of bourbon I'm dropping off to him."

"I gotta get back," Julia started to say, but I gave her a look. "Okay, Okay."

"I drove you here. In case you didn't notice, it's an hour and a half each way," I said. "I went with you, and now you are gonna stop with me for ten minutes while I go in to meet my client." Julia could test the patience of the Pope. "Have you not learned anything after that lunch? You can sit and act all high-and-mighty now, but I remember you working at the Club Bare Minimum in the French Quarter trying to make ends meet after you left the telecom job," I said, and Julia looked shocked. "You might have more in common with Donna Twilight than you care to admit from what those guys told us about her at lunch."

I pulled off the highway and parked in front of a building similar to the one we had just left. Julia sat looking at her hands and saying nothing. "You can sit in the car or you can come inside and sit in the waiting room while I meet with my client for ten or fifteen minutes." I took the keys out of the ignition and headed inside.

Chapter Thirteen

I BROUGHT A bottle of Gentleman Jack as a holiday thank you for my client. He had mentioned often enough after a long conference call that he was off to have a Jack and Coke after some of our brutal days slogging through reprogramming data gone wrong. Five minutes into the meeting with my client, I could have sworn I heard a car horn honking. Julia had opted to wait in the car. I'm sure she thought that would hurry me along. If it was Julia blowing the horn, I was going to pull her out of my vehicle by her hair right here and she could get home however she had to. My client jumped up to his feet saying it was probably one of his employees who bumped his new little roadster and set off the hair trigger on his car alarm. I wished him a happy holiday and headed back to my car.

My cell phone rang and it was Dante.

"Hey, I'm on a lunch break so I have a few minutes to talk," he said when I answered.

"Dante, I'm getting ready to drive back to New Orleans with Julia in my car. I'm in Houma, and I only have a few minutes to chat."

"What are you doing down there?" he asked. "With Julia?"

"It's a long story, and it has to do with Julia's brother who died at the party she had at her house the other night. Didn't Hanky and Taylor fill you in?"

"You met Taylor?"

"Yes, did they tell you about her brother?"

"Well, yeah, Julia's in it again," he said with the sound of exasperation in his voice. Dante and Julia could only agree on one thing and that was there was no love lost between them.

"No, I don't think so. But you're in Houston still, right?"

"Yes, I told you I probably won't get back till late Christmas Day, if at all. The flights are oversold."

"I need you to ask your pals in the Houston Police Department if they ever heard of this name and possible alias. I'm going to text it to you. See if you can get someone to run it. You're right there. It has to do with Julia's brother who died. Can you do that for me?"

"Get Hanky and Taylor to run them," he said in his ever-so-helpful tone.

"These names should pop in the Houston database. It's one name with an alias. Please?"

"All right. Text them to me. I'll call you if I get a hit or something on them, but if I do, I'm also going to give it to Hanky and Taylor. It's their case," he said and hung up.

"Merry Christmas," I said out loud to a dial tone. I continued, "Gee, Dante, sorry I'll miss you and your family this Christmas Eve. After all, it's only been every year since I was born that we've spent Christmas together with both our families at your house. But, don't worry about me. I've made other plans."

One of the things Dante did that annoyed me the most was hanging up without ever saying goodbye. Well, anyone who did it annoyed me, but he did it all the time, and while I didn't talk over the phone with him often, he was batting a thousand. Working in the telecommunications wheelhouse, I tried to impart this common phone courtesy which was totally lost on him. I knew I had made plans with Jiff at his parents' home. I just wanted Dante to realize I wasn't waiting for him anymore, and I wanted this painful squeezing of my heart to stop every time I thought about it.

I started to hit send after texting in the names Andre told us he knew Donna Twilight by, then I remembered something Larry said and added two more names and a phone number.

"Who was that?" Julia asked when I returned to the car.

"Dante," I said while texting the same information to Hanky.

"What did he want?" Julia asked. "I thought things were over with you two?"

"Well, wait, let me finish this text." I was looking at my phone and punched a few more names and a brief text explanation into my cell. I didn't want to call Hanky and explain it to her with Julia sitting right next to me.

"What?" I looked up and remembered she asked me about Dante. "Well, yes, I have made other plans this year with Jiff. I don't think I'm seeing him or his family, but Dante hasn't signed off on our relationship yet. This is hard, Julia."

"Dante hasn't signed off? It looks to me like he never signed on. He's never there for you," she said.

"You're right, but it doesn't stop me from wanting him to be there for me. I know it's what I'll never have," I said. "He just told me he's in Houston at a conference, and he won't be back for Christmas Eve. I didn't tell him I have other plans since I haven't heard from him in weeks. The last time we spoke was before Thanksgiving, and I didn't see him then either."

"I thought you have plans to spend Christmas Eve with Jiff at his parents' home?" Julia asked.

"Yes, but I've spent every Christmas Eve since I was born at Dante's house. My family goes there too, but the special part was being at his house with his family. You know how my mother is," I said.

"Yeah. If your family is always there, then why, why, why do you want to keep doing that?" Julia asked.

"Because, on Christmas Eve at Dante's house, his dad would bring home a real tree. It was a big tree, like ten-to-twelve-feet tall, since we all had homes with fourteen-foot ceilings." I said with that gooey, nostalgic feeling warming me. "It smelled so good, that fresh tree smell, all green and woodsy. Dante and his brothers helped him set it up and string the old-time colored lights on it. Then I'd help Dante and Mrs. Ruth put on her beautiful glass ornaments she collected over the years. Mrs. Ruth still makes fudge or other candy. When we were kids she would let us eat all we wanted when my mother wasn't looking. She made hot cocoa for the kids and Dante's dad made highballs for the adults. Sometimes my mother and sister would help decorate the tree."

"Your mother and sister were always there and you still liked it?" Julia asked.

"Well…yeah. When I was a kid, I didn't know any better yet," I said. My mother and sister are each an acquired taste I was still working to acquire.

Once we were headed home after stopping to see my client, I changed the subject off of Dante and me. I asked Julia about the people who came to the party I didn't get to meet. I wanted to know about the church ladies and asked her what possessed her to join that group.

"I felt I needed to go back to church because I have been fortunate lately with the bed and breakfast, and I thought it would help me become more understanding of people," Julia said.

"In that case, I think you need a new church to help you with understanding, because this one seems to have failed you…miserably."

"Very funny," she said.

"How did you get so chummy with them so fast," I asked, "because it does seem like these are your very new BFFs. Are some of them from the church group in your cooking club?"

"I joined the cooking group because I like to cook. Yes, some church ladies are gourmet cooking club members," Julia said. "Well, they call themselves that, even though their idea of a good meal is a potluck dinner."

"Cooks, or gourmet cooks?" I asked.

"It started as a cooking club a hundred years ago. That old lady that is still the president never comes to a meeting. We decided to raise the bar and make it a gourmet cooking club," Julia said.

"*We* decided to raise the bar?" I asked. "You all should have just gone *to a bar*."

"Okay, I decided to change the name because their idea of a cooking club was to learn how to make chicken one hundred different ways," Julia said.

"So who are these people officially in the group?" I asked. "Are all the cooking club members from your church group?"

"Most are and one or two bring friends or neighbors when they feel like it, but not all of the church ladies are in the cooking club," she said. "They drift in and out. They come when they feel like it."

"What was the deal with the rum balls?" I asked.

"We were all supposed to make our recipe of rum balls and give a box to each member. It doubled as a recipe test and Secret Santa exchange. Only the president could give each of us a number to write on the bottom of our box so we could vote on the winner at the next meeting."

"How many boxes were there to vote on? Do you know?" I asked.

"Eight," Julia said. "But when Larry and Donna drove in from Baton Rouge three hours early, I sent them to go walk around the French Quarter to kill some time. Frank said they took a couple of boxes of rum balls with them. That sounds like Larry. If those women hated me before, they are gonna be really ticked off when they find out I can't vote on their rum balls."

I thought, maybe they will be happier if she doesn't get to vote on any.

"Did you tell that to the police?" I asked. "Did you tell them that a box or two of rum balls were consumed and are now somewhere in a French Quarter trash can and perhaps on their way to a landfill?"

"I think I did," Julia said, rummaging around in her purse until she pulled out a lipstick.

"You know something isn't adding up with those rum balls. You're sure there were only supposed to be eight boxes?"

"Yes," Julia said.

"The ninth box had to be a second box sent from someone who already delivered their box to the president, right? The one that was in your mailbox never got a number, and Frank said the other eight were all delivered at the same time, with numbers."

"Right. So what?"

"So, someone sent that box to you. It was meant for you. Frank hid it so no one tasted it or even knew about it except Jiff and me. Did you taste any of the rum balls in any box? I didn't."

"No, I didn't have any," Julia said. "I'll call that lady cop you don't like. I need to make sure she knows there should have been eight boxes and Larry took two that we will never find."

"I like Hanky. We just had a disagreeable start. She isn't an easy person to get to know," I said. "It should be interesting to see what they find in those rum balls that were sent to your house."

Julia pulled the passenger sun visor down to open the mirror. She was still talking through pursed lips applying Fabulous Red lipstick, a color she raved about. "You know Hanky looks a lot better now. Looks like she had a makeover or something."

"That's because she was wearing man pants," I said.

"What d'ya mean? She was wearing man pants?" Julia looked disgusted. "Are you saying she was buying her clothes at the Men's Wearhouse?" Julia laughed as she applied her lipstick then rubbed her lips together to even out the desired effect so the red would look fabulous.

"Yes, that is exactly where she said she bought her clothes," I answered checking the rear view mirror to see if I could change lanes. "I suggested some other places she should shop."

Julia started making this hmm, hmm, hmm sound when she thought something didn't run in a parallel universe with hers.

"Julia, what made you invite your brother to this party in the first place? After all the things you've told me about him, I didn't think you would invite him to a nice holiday get-together like you had planned," I said and tried to catch her reaction with a sideways glance.

"I just wanted to see if we could mend the bridge. We were going to have to work together regarding the inheritance our dad and mother left us. We didn't touch any of it or ask for our share after mother died because of how dear old dad was. Neither of us wanted to have anything to do with him, even if it was through attorneys," Julia said.

"Why didn't you get along with him? It sounds like you both had bad experiences growing up that should have made you closer," I said.

"I think Larry was turning into my dad the older he got. If he knew how much money we would inherit, I'm sure he would have been impossible to work with. My dad had a good size nest egg off the labor of my mother. She worked all those years, and daddy dearest made her save every cent she earned. She never got to spend any on herself. Once she bought a new dress, shoes, and a purse. When my dad came home and saw her wearing something new, he hit her," Julia said. "Larry never took up for our mother, not once."

"Julia, he was a kid too. It's hard to stand up to your parents, no matter how old you get," I said. "Those men Larry worked with sounded like they knew your brother pretty well. They knew he was lonely and that he picked out or went for, wait, how did they put it?"

"The broken one," Julia said.

"Maybe Larry wanted to help someone to make up for not being able to help you or your mother. Did you ever think of that?"

"No, I guess I didn't," Julia said. We rode in silence for awhile.

"How much is your inheritance?" I finally asked.

"It's over ten million dollars," Julia said, as if she just told me to pull over for gas at the next station.

"What?" I almost drove off the road thinking I heard wrong. "For real?"

"Yes. He was a penny pincher and lived like a hermit. I don't know where or when he thought he would start spending the money," she said. "He was like a hoarder. The service I sent to clean out his house after he died said they took over thirty industrial-size garbage bags out of his home stuffed with plastic grocery bags. He had them all separated by color; white ones, tan ones, blue ones."

"Did Larry know how much your inheritance was or did his wife?" I asked.

"I don't know. The attorney only told me Larry knew about it, but he wasn't sure if Donna knew. Larry said he married her after my dad died at City Hall about two weeks ago."

"What does the will say?" I asked still astounded by the amount.

"Mister Know-It-All didn't have a will," Julia said.

"No will? He had that much money and he didn't make a will?" I asked in disbelief. "Well, this state has definite laws pertaining to inheritance, with or without a will. You might want to ask Jiff."

"I guess my old man thought he was going to live forever. He was mean enough that I thought he was gonna live forever. Mean people don't die. They just get older and meaner," Julia said. "The attorney in Baton Rouge called the morning of the party to tell me what the estate was worth with the real estate, investments, and savings. I asked him not to tell Larry until I had a chance to talk to him. I planned on talking to him after the party. He apologized and said Larry had been by his office earlier on another matter unrelated to the inheritance issue, and the attorney told him what he was now telling me," Julia said. "So, Larry knew."

"Did the attorney give you any idea what Larry else wanted to see him about?" I asked.

"No, but I wonder how much Donna knows about all this—about Larry's share of the inheritance. The bigger question is: how much trouble is she going to be over it?" Julia said.

"Under Louisiana law, if he inherits money, she isn't entitled to it anyway unless they comingle the funds like in a joint account," I said. "Did Larry make a will? You need to check with that attorney to find out if Larry left her any in case he died first. I think it's called right of survivorship in case they both die at the same time. It outlines how money is inherited if there are no children involved."

Julia just shrugged by way of an answer. She was deep in thought and it seemed all of this was a lot, even for her to handle.

"If Donna did know about the inheritance, I wonder if she also knew how much," I said.

"I didn't know it was going to be that much. I don't think Larry did either. That was a surprise. I expected it to be a chunk of money since Scrooge saved every cent. He only called us to say happy birthday or merry Christmas. He was so cheap, he called so he didn't have to buy a card or stamp.

"There's no telling how much Donna Twilight knows," Julia went on. "Larry was no genius, but I bet he decided to keep her in the dark. He was shrewd when it came to money, his money. I didn't even know he was married until they showed up and told me three hours before the party. I found out about my inheritance two weeks ago and that was the day after he died. I guess that was enough time for Donna to arrange a wedding."

"Who else knew about the inheritance? Did you tell LB?" I asked.

"No. I didn't tell anyone. When I called Larry to invite him to the party, he told me he went to see Dad's attorney. He told me he knew about the inheritance, but he didn't mention whatever else he was there for. He didn't mention Donna or anyone he was about to marry, no matter what she calls herself," Julia said and pulled out her compact and applied more Fabulous Red lipstick.

I thought Julia or Larry had to have told someone else. That much money someone is about to inherit doesn't stay a secret for long. Frank knew and told me. I didn't want to snitch on Frank. Maybe Frank overhead Julia talking to Larry or LB. I'd have to ask him. Maybe Donna Twilight, aka Cherie Sassone, overheard Larry and told someone. Or she snooped through his things. Snooping. Isn't that what Frank said LB was doing when Julia wasn't home?

"I need to stop for gas," I said. "And you're paying."

Chapter Fourteen

T HE RIDE HOME with Julia flew by once she started talking. She told me about Patrick, the affair, and Sheila.

"Are you still seeing him after the flour incident?" I waited for an answer. I was determined not to make another sound until she answered me.

"Now and then," she said finally. "I know it isn't a good idea."

"Julia, why? He has nothing to offer you, and you are hurting another woman in the process. Sheila hasn't done anything to you, well except express her disapproval by distributing a ten-pound bag of Gold Seal Flour all over your kitchen. Was it the all-purpose one?"

"Ha. Ha."

"Think about it. You have been making a genuine effort to meet someone. You joined a dating service," I said.

Julia immediately started to complain about how much of a rip-off it had been, so I had to jump in adding, "Okay, I know that was a bust, but the point I'm trying to make is you've been making an effort to meet someone to have a relationship with. Patrick can't have that or give that to you. You were going to try speed dating to meet someone, and you did. You are only sabotaging yourself in relationships that can actually work by entertaining a married man."

"I know," was all she could say.

"We deserve better. I feel like I could mess up this thing with Jiff every time I hear Dante's name or his voice. You and I deserve to be happy, and we need to find the man who wants to be happy with us. We really need to support each other in this," I said. "Not just you and I, but other women looking for what we're looking for."

"You are right," she said. "Sometimes, I'm my own worst enemy."

"You had a good day today. You learned good things about your brother. All those men really liked him and enjoyed working with him. He looked out for you in case something happened to him. He even tried to help Donna, Cherie, whatever her real name is. You heard what kind of life she came from."

"I need to find out more about that marriage and the reason Larry met with my dad's attorney," Julia said.

I was thinking the same thing.

🍸 🍸 🍸

THE REST OF the drive was uneventful and we rode in silence. I was going over in my head all the work I had to wrap up at the office and the Christmas cards I had to finish addressing so I could mail them. I still needed to buy gift certificates for my mother and sister. Since my sister was pregnant, I decided to get her a gift certificate at a baby store that also sold maternity clothing. If there had been a book called *The Art of the Never-ending Complaint*, it would have been a perfect gift for my mother. No matter what I got her, she wasn't going to like it and she would ask where to return it. I decided to give her a gift card from a major credit card company she could use anywhere. I know she has a MasterCard so that's it. Done. I had already bought my dad the power tool he dropped a thousand hints at wanting—something called a jigsaw.

Also gnawing on my subconscious were the nine gold foil boxes of rum balls. Then I remembered what Agnes told me and it hit me. I had to call Hanky.

I dropped Julia off and made a phone call to Hanky. I told Hanky it didn't matter what the tox screen said about the boxes of rum balls. The rum balls were not the cause of death. I told her to have the toothpicks checked. Then I headed to pick up the last two items I needed for Christmas gifts and stopped at my parents' home to drop off the presents I bought for my family and Woozie.

I pulled up to my parents' home and there was a large, blow up stork wearing a Santa hat and holding a baby in a sling. Great. I don't suppose they are worried the neighbors would start counting on their fingers from the date of the wedding to now to see if my sister, Sherry, was pregnant before they got married. The neighbors always seemed to know everyone's business anyway, so I guess my family is past that point of concern.

Only Woozie was home and I found her in the kitchen doing what she does best, cooking. Woozie had been with my dad's mother as a cook and housekeeper, then she took care of my dad when he married, much to my mother's dismay. Woozie makes it very clear she is here for my dad, not my mother. If I ever get married and have my own home, I'm hoping Woozie is still going strong enough to take care of us.

"Wha' you mean you not comin' here for Christmas Eve?" Woozie asked, right after she wheeled around from the pot she was stirring on the stove and stood with both hands on her hips, still holding a big wooden spoon. I was sitting at the kitchen table. "I'm makin' all the things you and your daddy like. I'm makin' the turkey, cornbread stuffin', oyster stuffin', my biscuits you love, and I got a Kringle for your dessert."

Wow, she was pulling out all the stops.

"I have other plans. I've been invited to go to Jiff's parents' home for Christmas Eve, and I accepted the invitation," I said and tried to take a sip of the fresh coffee Woozie made for me. "That's why I'm dropping off your gifts today, so all of you have them to open."

"You lucky yo' momma and sister be out shoppin' for da baby, cuz dey sure not gonna be happy to hear dis," Woozie said, still standing with hands on her hips, only now the spoon was dripping on the floor.

"When do you worry about making my mother happy? She and Sherry are so wrapped around the baby coming they won't care," I said. "They're buying more baby gifts? It looks like there's about a hundred wrapped under the tree already to Baby Alexander Deedler, my grandbaby, our first little angel, and on and on. Why do they even wrap them when the baby isn't even here yet?" I asked Woozie. "Besides, you and I both know my mother won't miss me for a second."

"But yo' daddy will. Dis gonna break his heart. He gonna be next door at da Deedlers wit out you for da first time since you were a baby just home from da hospital. Hmm, hmm, hmm," Woozie said and turned back to stir the pot.

"You know in my heart I always wanted things to work out with Dante. I haven't heard from him since before Thanksgiving. If you recall, no one seemed to miss me here at Thanksgiving when I was at Jiff's house for dinner," I said.

"Dante Deedler ain't talked to you since Thanksgiving?" Woozie asked. "Mens."

"It's been more like since Halloween. I just talked to him yesterday and he told me that he was in Houston for a meeting, and when the conference is over, the return flights to New Orleans are completely full. He might have to wait until Christmas night to get back," I said. "This is so typical of him. He waits until the last minute to tell me he hasn't planned anything or has something else he has to do. Its Christmas. Don't you think he knew this at least a week ago?"

"Mens," Woozie said again, shaking her head. This was Woozie's catchall phrase for what any man did to her, to me, to her sister, to any woman, that we did not understand. "Now I see why you don't wanna go over there. But yo' daddy is gonna be brokenhearted, you mark my words. Besides, he wants to see you, not the Deedlers or the gift you bought him."

"None of that matters anyway. I have other plans with Jiff and his family for Christmas Eve," I said. "What about you? Do you wanna know what I got you for Christmas?"

"Woozie don't care what you buys for her." Woozie used the third person when she was terribly interested in anything I had to tell her or give her.

"Well, you're gonna be with Silas and your family, and I have some gifts for you to bring to them," I taunted her by pulling up a big Macy's shopping bag full of professionally wrapped gifts in Macy's boxes with Macy's bows.

"Like what?" Woozie feinted noninterest but turned to see what was in the shopping bag. She stopped stirring the pot and left the spoon in it. If something took Woozie away from anything to do with food or cooking, it had to be good. She took a step toward me to see what might be coming out of the Macy's bags I had hauled in with me.

"Like a new hat, gloves, and matching scarf to go with the new winter coat I bought you." I made a grand gesture of putting the overflowing bag in the center of the table. She had complained for weeks her old coat "had done had it" and she didn't have time to go shop for a new one. Then she said she was going to wait until everything went on sale after Christmas. By then, I thought she might not find her size. Woozie was a tall, big woman. Even without heels she towered over me. If I had to guess, Woozie was at least six foot five in bare feet.

"What? A new coat? Brandy girl, you don't need to go spendin' your hard earn money on Woozie," she said and started opening the smaller of the gifts. "What' dis? Dis don't feel like no coat."

"That's the surprise gift," I said. It was a new handbag to complete her winter ensemble. "Dere's money in dis here purse," Woozie said, opening it immediately and seeing the cash.

"Well, that's for shoes to go with your new coat and accessories. You might want a nice pair to wear with the coat to go to church. I didn't think I could find the shoes you would like, so there's some cash, and besides, all purses should come with some money in them for good luck," I said. The truth about the shoes was I would never attempt to buy Woozie shoes since she had the biggest feet on the planet, and I knew I'd never find a pair to fit her, let alone be comfortable. She wore very wide, very big flat shoes. She was on her own to find a nice pair of shoes.

"You spent too much on Woozie. You return all dis and get your hard earn money back," Woozie said.

"No can do, Wooz. I bought it all on sale, and all sales are final," I said. It wasn't true one bit about being on sale, but it was one of those little white lies we learned in catechism as kids.

"I'm glad you didn't buy me no shoes. You probably only shop for shoes where you buy dose high heels things you always be wearing. Don't you know any stores dat sell flat, comfortable shoes in your size?"

Woozie was opening the large box with the coat and then proceeded to try it on. "This fits Woozie perfect." She had put on the hat which was a cloche like she always wore, but this one had a large, pretty silk flower on the side. Everything was a beautiful, dark burgundy which Woozie referred to as dubonnet—French for a sweet, red wine similar in color. She opened and put on the matching gloves, the scarf, and was holding the handbag as she walked back and forth in the kitchen showing me how she looked in them.

"You look like a fashionista in your new things," I said and gave her a hug and a kiss.

"I look like what?" she asked.

"A fashionista. It's a good thing."

"Oh, I know it's a good thing cuz I feels good in dese. I'm glad dey was all on sale. I just wanna tell all my friends that you, Brandy girl, made Woozie a fashionista," she said, smiling from ear to ear.

Woozie was always more like a mother to me than my own mother. My sister, Sherry, was clearly my mother's favorite, and all who came in contact with her knew it because she told them. And I quote, "Sherry is my favorite, and its too bad Brandy isn't more like her."

Nice.

"I've got to get back to work. Here's gifts for the rest of your family," I said, handing her another shopping bag. "Tell all of them I love them, and Merry Christmas from me."

She grabbed me and gave me a smothering bear hug, burying my face into her bosom the size of which I had never seen a bra in any store to fit. As kids, my sister and I saw Woozie's underwear when she used our washing machine on days she cleaned. We called them ten-gallon brassieres. It made me wonder who makes them in this size.

Chapter Fifteen

F RANK CALLED WHILE I was at work trying to manage a
team of people to divide and conquer a boatload of data
we had to go through and find where the money was going
out of the company.

"The police have all the results of the rum balls, and
they're coming over here in about an hour. Can you be here?"
he asked.

"Does Julia know you're calling me?" I asked.

"Yes, she's calling LB and asking him to come over as
well," he said.

"Did the police ask for LB to be there?" I asked.

"I don't think so," Frank said. "The Queen is screaming
for me. Can you come?" he asked.

"Yes, I'll be there," I said, and then he hung up. Ah, the
Dante school of phone etiquette.

DRIVING TO JULIA'S, all I could think about was everything
seemed to hinge on two weeks. Julia met LB two weeks ago.
Larry married Donna Twilight, aka Cherie Sassone, two
weeks ago. Larry and Julia found out about their inheritance
two weeks ago, the day after their father died. The Houma

branch where Larry worked said he came in about two weeks ago to name his beneficiary, and it was Julia, not his new wife.

Hanky and Taylor's unmarked car was parked in the front, and they were already inside. I pulled into the driveway and parked. I got out of my BMW and walked up the side of the guesthouse facing Janice and Ned's house. One, two, three windows back from the front, I noticed a solitary bush with all the leaves fallen off and on the ground. All that was left were long, slender branches the size of a fat toothpick in diameter. Many of the smaller branches had been recently cut. There were dried leaves on the mound at the base of the plant.

I entered the guesthouse through the back door and found Detectives Hanky and Taylor in the double parlor with Julia and Frank. They waved me in and Detective Taylor began with what forensics found on the rum ball boxes, or rather what they didn't find.

"The rum balls themselves did not contain poison," Detective Taylor said. "There were, however, other added ingredients in the unnumbered box to suggest that foul play was intended, but not murder."

Julia and I looked at each other.

"What do you mean, foul play intended but not murder?" Julia asked.

Detective Taylor was very matter-of-fact when he said, "In the unmarked, unnumbered box left in your mailbox, there was saltpeter in the rum balls. Inconvenient to your male guests but not lethal."

"Saltpeter?" I said. "I'm betting on Bicky or Sheila."

Detective Hanky continued, "Sheila. Her prints were on that box. She's a school teacher so her prints are in the system."

"As far as the other marked boxes, there was a high percentage of laxatives in two boxes, and since that might be a secret ingredient in the recipe, we had to let those go," Taylor said. "Since we don't know which two Larry took to the French Quarter, by process of elimination we feel that it was two of the numbered boxes unaccounted for."

Hanky added, "But in the two boxes your brother ate from here, forensics identified oleander twigs as being used to spear the food, like a toothpick. There were also crushed oleander leaves found in one box the rum balls appeared to be rolled in. It was a numbered box, but we think the leaves were added, like the twig toothpicks, after they were delivered here. According to the president of your cooking club, one of the boxes with the toothpicks was hers, and she claims not to have put anything in the box except rum balls. She also said she personally checked all the boxes that were delivered here and nothing other than a dozen rum balls were in each box, no twigs, no leaves. They were delivered here by the ninety-year-old president's grandson on his bike. We questioned her and we don't believe she added oleander leaves or twigs. No motive."

"Oleander?" Julia asked. "Oleander is poisonous."

"Right. It seems whoever put oleander twigs in the boxes or rolled the rum balls in the crushed leaves knew that," Hanky said, looking at Julia. "Forensics concluded your brother ate a lot of rum balls with oleander from the results of his stomach contents."

"You need to talk to my brother's wife. She was the one spearing them with the twigs. I had no idea it was oleander she was using," Julia said.

"Larry even asked Julia if she put the twigs in the box he was eating from," I said. "We were standing right there. I saw him eat the twig with the rum ball. Julia told him that it wasn't her box of rum balls he was eating from with twigs."

"If any of us had known it was oleander, we would have stopped him. We know its poisonous. Heck, you can poison yourself just by handling it or burning the leaves," Julia said.

Hanky, Taylor, Julia, and I looked back and forth at each other. It dawned on all of us at the same time that Donna Twilight had been touching the twigs and feeding Larry. If she was involved with giving Larry the oleander, she might not have known handling it could poison her.

"I saw Donna go fetch the twigs from the box Larry polished off to use them in the next box he started eating," I said. "They were sitting in the dining room at the table. Jiff and I walked past the sideboard checking out the desserts and cheeses. Jiff and I watched Larry practically force feed Donna a rum ball, but then I saw her spit it out into a napkin when he wasn't looking. When the carolers started singing, we went outside to ask them to leave early since we were about to sit down for dinner."

"Ms. Richard, we have to ask. Did you cut any oleander and put it in those boxes of rum balls your brother consumed or ask any of your staff to cut oleander for you?" Detective Taylor asked.

"Me? Look, my brother and I had our differences, but no, I didn't want to see him dead. I didn't ask Frank or anyone to cut oleander or anything outside. I had flowers for my party delivered," Julia said. She looked thoughtful like she remembered something. She added, "As far as my staff, that's only Frank, and I'm not even sure Frank knows an oleander bush from a rose bush."

Frank was uncommonly quiet. I gave Hanky the eye movement that means "meet me in the hall" and she left Taylor to continue asking Julia questions.

In the hall I told Hanky, "I just remembered that Janice told me she saw LB, Julia's boyfriend, cutting on a bush the day of Julia's party. She told me that at the feed and seed store dog party. She thought Julia had him pruning her landscape. Janice said she thought it odd that he was only pruning one bush and it was under the third window from the street. On the way in here, I went to the third window and the bush she saw him pruning is an oleander bush."

"Show me the bush," Hanky said.

We went out the back door in the kitchen so that the others wouldn't see us leave. As we made our way around the back and up the side, Hanky asked me what each bush or shrub was Julia had planted along the house. "I don't know the names of them, but I know they are not oleander," I said. "Most of these along the back and side are azaleas."

"What's this one?" Hanky asked.

"Not oleander," I said as Hanky stopped at every bush and asked what it was. I didn't want to give her a horticultural lesson on every shrub in the garden.

"What's this?" she asked of the fifth or six plant.

"Really? You can't tell that flower is a rose? That would make it a rose bush?" I said. "Even with the dead blooms you can see they are roses."

"What's this? It's red, so it's that Christmas plant…point something," Hanky said very proud of herself.

"That's a poinsettia. If you eat it, it might make you sick, but I don't think it's considered poisonous." The plant was a good eight-to-ten-feet tall covered in blooms. It was beautiful and one of the few, if not the only flowering plant outside.

"Here. Here is the oleander bush, almost a tree now. See, it's under the third window from the front, and look across the street," I said, turning to face Janice and Ned's house. I did a low wave back at the house so my arm wasn't flailing all over drawing attention to us. "I see Janice at her window watching us."

"I bet she knows more of what goes on here than the ones living here do," Hanky said. "She won't miss much from that viewpoint. That's better than most stakeouts."

We were right under the window of the double parlor and could hear Detective Taylor still questioning Julia while Frank looked on, pulling at the hair on the back of his head. I'm sure they could see the top of my head if they looked out. I stooped over to keep my head out of view.

Hanky was short, so she looked at me and asked, "Why are you standing like that?"

"I don't want them to see me out here. You'd need a ladder if you want them to see you," I said. I tried not to move around much so we didn't draw attention to ourselves.

"Check this out," Hanky said after scrutinizing the oleander bush we were standing next to. She pointed to a couple of the slender, spiny branches with clean cuts across them.

"That's what Janice said. She told me this LB, boyfriend-guy was out here cutting on this bush."

"Yes, but that doesn't prove he was the only one cutting it," she said. "How many of these trees or bushes are all over this neighborhood?" Hanky started looking around.

We stood there a minute trying to see if there were others in our line of sight. I thought Janice had one in her yard, but we needed to take a closer look.

"Didn't you speak with Agnes, the president of the gourmet cooking club?" I asked Hanky. "I gave you her number. She told me she checked every box. That means those boxes—all those boxes, even the unnumbered one left in the mailbox—came to this house without those toothpicks in them Larry was so gung ho over."

Finally, Hanky said, "We need to question boyfriend LB again."

Hanky had been referring to Julia's male friends as boyfriend LB or boyfriend married man.

"Look, I have a strange feeling about him. I can't say why yet. I didn't speak to him past the introduction at the front door the night of the party. I haven't seen him here since, and that's odd, don't you think?" I asked her. "It was his idea to take Donna Twilight to the ER and not wait for the ambulance."

"He's not staying here is he?" Hanky asked.

"No, but you knew that," I said, giving her a sideways look.

"Just checking to see if there was a status change," Hanky said.

"No. According to Frank he's still at the Fairmont Hotel near the hospital where Donna Twilight is. Julia says LB goes to the hospital every day, and she's happy with the fact that she doesn't have to go see her," I said.

"As if Julia would take time to visit the sick," Hanky muttered.

"I know it's Julia, but it's strange and weird if you think about it. If LB is Julia's boyfriend, why isn't he here to support Julia? Why is he spending so much time with Donna Twilight?" I asked.

"Well, you are good at seeing things other people miss," Hanky said. "What do you think? LB's hot for Donna? That would track because even if she's a stripper…"

"Exotic dancer," I said cutting Hanky off.

"Whatever. Even if she's… an exotic dancer, she has to be infinitely nicer than Julia," Hanky said.

"LB told Julia he's some sort of trust fund baby who manages his family's investment interests. If that's true, why is he hovering over Donna Twilight? Why isn't he hovering over Julia who stands to inherit a boatload of money her dad left her and the brother," I said.

I saw Hanky's attention skyrocket when I said inheritance. "I know, I know it looks suspicious that the brother who is supposed to inherit along with Julia is offed, and now Julia is left to receive it all. But does Donna Twilight know that? And, why is a guy who supposedly has big bucks, I'm talking about LB now, speed dating? Women, all women, should be lined up trying to persuade him into calling them," I said.

Hanky was thinking for a few moments then asked me, "Do you think LB and Donna know each other from somewhere else?"

"I do. I also don't think LB is from Colorado which is why I asked Dante to run their names while he's in Houston," I said. "I asked him when he called me yesterday to tell me—again—he will miss Christmas with our families this year.”

“Boo-Hoo for you,” Hanky said. “You have a hot guy on standby. I don’t think you’ll be alone or have a Blue, Blue, Blue, Blue Christmas,” she said singing the last part. Then she added, “But Dante will.”

I did my best to hide my aggravation at Hanky’s unrequited devotion to Dante. “The reason I’m telling you this is because I asked Dante to run an 800 phone number that Julia said LB uses and a couple of names Donna Twilight might be known as while he’s in Houston and ask around if Houston PD knows them. Julia’s brother said he met Donna in Houston when he was there on business. Larry said it was at a club with speed dating on one of his business trips,” I said. “I think LB has more of a Texas accent than a Colorado one, if there is such an accent. Also, Larry mentioned he knew or thought LB was from Colorado at the party as soon as they met. Maybe Donna Twilight told Larry that LB was from Colorado, because I’m not sure Julia even knew.”

“I think you told me LB said he met Julia speed dating, didn’t you?” Hanky asked.

“Right. They went somewhere here in New Orleans to speed date, met in the bar before it started, and left. That was about two weeks ago. The two-week timeframe keeps gnawing at me.

“I think that’s too much of a coincidence. Dante said he’d give you and Taylor the info if he found out anything,” I said. “Why would he go to a speed dating place here if he lives somewhere else?”

Hanky said, "I think Taylor and I need to go question LB and the strip…," Hanky caught herself and finished, "wife again."

Chapter Sixteen

I WOKE UP, early—very early—worrying about everything. Today was Wednesday. That left Thursday and half a day on Friday to finish all things work related, shopping, wrapping up my Christmas gifts to Jiff and his family, and make my signature rum balls to hand out to friends and work associates. I made a mental note to stop and get Kringles for anyone associated with the recent debacle at Julia's. I thought rum balls might be too 'in your face.'

Julia's distractions since her party last Friday had me woefully behind. I had several files open on my desk, and I'd be there late or should be there late tonight to make sure the customers were protected and the information was sent to the proper authorities to investigate. My office party was Thursday after work and Jiff's party was Friday afternoon. Christmas Eve was Saturday night. I closed my eyes and did a silent scream to myself, so if Suzanne was home I wouldn't wake her. Sometimes a silent scream helped with the stress of work. It didn't always help when I had to deal with Julia, like now. When I opened my eyes, Meaux was looking at me with his head cocked to one side. I guess he was wondering why he couldn't figure out what I was saying.

I still had rum balls to make, and they had to be made soon so the rum could sit and smooth out. They needed at least a day. Two days were better so they didn't taste like a straight shot of booze. My rum balls needed to mature or people would choke on them. I decided to make them this morning before I left for work, otherwise another day would go by and I'd be that much further behind.

The other big thing breathing down my neck was I did not have a gift for Jiff yet. I thought about buying him a Mont Blanc pen but then I saw he had one. So did Detective Taylor for that matter, not that I planned on getting him a gift. I had rum balls for him and Hanky.

I had bought Isabella the gift of a pet bed for when she came to visit us. It was from Meaux. He also had some toys for her, but he was in the habit of tearing the wrapping off of them. I had rewrapped them so many times, I finally moved them from under the tree to a higher place where he could not get to them. Then he started to lay in Isabella's pet bed even though it was wrapped.

"Dude," I said to Meaux, "what are we gonna get Jiff for Christmas? The man has everything, and if he doesn't already have it, he can buy a lot nicer one than we could ever afford to buy for him." Meaux just looked at me, and I could tell he was pondering the question. He was standing in Isabella's bed on top of the gift wrap. When he moved, the sound of paper rustling gave him away. "You know you're wrinkling the gift wrap and poking tiny holes in it when you walk on it, right?" He barked once as if in agreement. Gift wrap was not important to Meaux, and his idea of a gift for Jiff was probably something chicken or beef flavored.

I called and left messages for my staff on what to do this morning in order to get me ready to review the files I was working on. That would save some time, and I said I'd be in by ten thirty.

Rolling rum balls allowed me time to think. It was therapeutic. I couldn't run from place to place trying to get more done than I had time to do it in.

I thought about having promised Woozie to stop and see my dad on Christmas Eve. It was the first Christmas I wasn't living at home and next door to Dante's family. I was ready for a change. Stopping there might put me in a nostalgic mood before I went to Jiff's house, and I didn't want anything spoiling that. In the short time I had known his parents and siblings, they made me feel included. Dante's parents made me feel included even when Dante wasn't there. I was tired of trying to get Dante to include me in his life.

I packed a tin with rum balls and wrote on the gift tag *To: Dante's Family, From Brandy*. When I finished putting all the rum balls in gift tins, I put the tins in a big Macy's shopping bag to transport them. Then, when I made my rounds on Christmas Eve to the vet, hairdresser, landlord, and the office to give one to each of the staff, they were ready to go. I signed my name with Meaux's paw print on the gift tags to the vet, my friends, and the landlord. The one to Isabella was signed "Love and Licks from Meaux."

I asked him, "Meaux, did I forget any of your friends?"

He barked.

"Oh right. Isabella's dad, that would be Jiff, should get his own tin of rum balls after all I put him through with this fiasco," I said.

Everyone would want to leave early Friday, and by the afternoon most would have skedaddled out of there to start his or her holiday early by either cooking or getting travel plans underway to visit family.

Just the idea of having a clear schedule by Friday afternoon helped me relax a little, and the idea of what to get Jiff as a Christmas gift popped into my head. It was perfect. If I finished the rum balls by ten o'clock, I could run into a store on the way to the office and grab a nice one. And, it would let him know that I was ready for our life to move forward together.

I went back to rolling rum balls and thinking. My cell phone rang and I didn't want to answer it, but I saw it was Dante. While caller ID indicated he was calling, another call from Hanky was coming in also.

No, no, no. I had too much to do and getting involved this early on the last full day I had to get everything done in was not a good idea.

The next thing was a text from Dante saying *I know you can see this is me calling you. It's important. Pick up the phone.* Then it started ringing again. He must have called Hanky first if she was calling me too. I knew it had to do with Julia and the suspicious death of her brother. This call was not a heartfelt explanation on how much he was going to miss me on Christmas Eve.

I managed to use my knuckle to answer it on the last ring before the call went to voice mail again, and since my hands were full of rum ball mix, I had to use speakerphone. "Yes?"

"Am I on speakerphone? Take me off of it."

"Yes, you are and no, I can't. No one is here but me, and I'm making rum balls so my hands are full of the mix," I said.

Dante plodded right into his business for calling me without mentioning how much he liked my rum balls or would miss them. "You asked me to look up something, and I have info on it." Dante sounded annoyed with me.

"You could have left it on voice mail if I'm keeping you from something," I said.

"I've got something on those names you gave me to run. Stay away from those two. They're bad news. LB Sutton has a laundry list of aliases and addresses in almost every state. He's a hustler and hustles women out of money or expensive jewelry. No telling how many have had money stolen by him because many are too embarrassed to come forward," Dante said.

"Any photos of him?" I asked.

"No, he seems to move on rather fast. His name pops up from Texas to Colorado on cases where he's wanted for questioning," he said.

"Colorado?" I asked.

"Talk to Hanky, she's got it all. I'm due back in this conference," he said, and I heard the loudspeaker making the announcement to return to your seat. "Look, I know you're upset over me not calling over the last couple of weeks, and…."

"I'm not upset." I said, but my rum balls were being rolled smaller and smaller. I thought if I squeezed them any tighter they would turn into diamonds.

"Hanky said you mentioned it was the first Christmas we wouldn't spend at my parents' home. I hadn't realized that, but the promotion came late and this conference was full, so it made it hard to get airfare back in time…" he said and I cut him off again.

"It is what it is. You and Hanky have more conversations about relationships, ours included, than you and I ever had. You should talk to Hanky about this." I didn't want to get into it over the phone, and I was sorry I had said that. I stopped rolling the rum balls. I grabbed the bottle and took a swallow of 180 proof Jamaican rum. My eyes starting running water and I thought I might self-combust.

There was a long pause, mainly because I was still feeling the burn from the rum, and an involuntary cough helped clear my throat.

"I don't know what to say," Dante mumbled.

I cleared my throat again and discovered I could still speak. "Dante, you never know what to say. I've hung onto your every unspoken word for years. This Christmas has made me realize that I will always be waiting for you to say the right thing, to ask the right thing, to say something, anything that involves you and me. Merry Christmas, Dante. I'll drop some rum balls off at your parents' house."

I hung up without saying goodbye.

Chapter Seventeen

I THOUGHT ABOUT calling Frank to see if Donna Twilight or Cherie, whatever her name is, was ever released from the hospital and returned to the guesthouse. I decided to just call the hospital myself.

When I asked to be transferred to her room I was put on hold. The hospital operator came back a few minutes later and said there was no one named Donna Richard admitted. I then asked if maybe it was under her maiden name of Donna or Cherie Sassone.

Again, she put me on hold, which should be re-named the Ignore Button, since I often feel that's what is happening.

She returned and said no one with either name had been admitted or released. I asked if she could look her up by date of admission or the reason why she was brought in. She must have been new or in the holiday spirit because normally no one will give out that information on a patient over the phone. I was put on hold again for a few minutes and when she returned she said, "We had a patient brought into the emergency unit on Friday night believed to have ingested a poison. Would that be her?"

"Yes, I think it is," I said.

"She was released earlier today and her husband checked her out," the operator said.

"Her husband? He was also poisoned, but…." I stopped myself. "That's right. She was recently married, just two weeks ago. I guess she used his name."

"She must have to check out. She checked in under Donna Richard and checked out as Donna Sutton."

I CALLED HANKY to see if she knew what was going on and if she knew about the interesting name Donna was now using.

"Your friend, the exotic dancer, she's been arrested for several crimes like hustling men for money and lewd behavior. All misdemeanors. No convictions," Hanky said.

"Arrested for prostitution?" I asked.

"No. She hustles them, acting like she's going with them because she's interested. Meets most of them speed dating. She never talks money or a service. Kinda smart if you think about it. Keeps a prostitution arrest out of it. Then she slips them something in their drink, takes their money, and leaves a note with a big kiss on it saying what a great time she had, hope she sees him again the next time he travels through," Hanky said.

"Looks and sounds consensual," I said.

"Right," Hanky said. "And I bet she takes a photo of him passed out with the note so if she gets charged, the wife will see what hubby's been up to. That would keep most of them from wanting to file charges."

"Houston PD thinks she has an accomplice. They all happened at a string of bars from here to Texas—well actually to Houma, not New Orleans—that some group owns. They are in LLCs and have other LLCs buy and sell them, so it's hard to find out who actually owns them."

"It's LB," I said. "The guy who owns them is going to be LB."

"I don't know. Dante ran LB's name and there's no warrants on him. He seems to be wanted for questioning over missing jewelry in California and Colorado." Hanky said. "Those bars from here to Houston are honky tonks, exotic dancer-type bars, the likes of which Donna Twilight would work in. Has LB tried to hustle Julia or ask for money yet?"

"No," I said. "But I'd like to know how he bought her that bracelet. Now it makes sense why LB was so attentive to Donna in the hospital. She might be his cash cow on the speed dating circuit and a victim in all this too."

"Doubt that. Donna Twilight has made the rounds from Houma to Houston. She's more of a willing participant than a victim. Taylor and I need to find LB to question him again. He checked out of the Fairmont and Donna Twilight checked out of University Hospital," she said.

"Did you know she used LB's last name to check out of the hospital?" I asked.

"Yes and we're looking into that. I'm hoping she's a bigamist. Then we have something else to arrest her for if she was married to LB when she married Julia's brother," Hanky said. "Donna doesn't strike me as the sharpest tool in the shed. A hustler—yes, the brain trust—no."

"Check at Julia's. I bet they went there to stay," I said. "LB asked Julia if Donna could stay for a week or two until Larry was buried. See. He's looking out for Donna. I have to drop off a Christmas gift to Julia and Frank. Let me ask if either of them knows where they are. I'll call you or text you if I find out anything."

"I hope you're not bringing them rum balls," Hanky said.

"No, but it's not a bad idea to give them to LB and Donna," I laughed. "Julia might not find it amusing. I have Kringles for them." I said and hung up. I was annoyed with myself when I realized I didn't say goodbye. It didn't matter, Hanky would never notice. Besides, I had a tin of rum balls for Hanky and Taylor. A little homicide humor for the holidays.

WHEN I PULLED up in front of Julia's mansion, a car was in the drive with an insurance logo for Lloyds's of London on it. I sat in my car and called the bed and breakfast from my cell phone. Frank answered and he sounded hysterical.

"Please come here now," Frank begged.

"I'm sitting out front," I said.

"Then please get in here," he said. "Now."

"I have to get to work. Pa-le-e-e-e-ze, Frank," I begged. "Can you run out and get this Kringle for you and Julia?"

"No. You need to come in." Frank was sniffling now and the waterworks were going to start. Did I even want to know what was going on?

"Frank, is LB there? Have you or Julia heard from LB and Donna Twilight?"

"He's supposed to be here now, but he's late," Frank said. "There are two people here from the insurance company about Julia's bracelet. They're asking me all kinds of questions, and she's not home. They think I stole it. It's missing. Her bracelet is missing," Frank said between sobs. "And I'm going to be arrested."

"Please calm down, Frank. I need you to do something. This will all clear up soon," I said.

"What?" Frank stopped to blow his nose in what I could only assume was one of his man hankies. "What do you want me to do?"

"Don't let them leave, but see if they will move their car before LB gets there. Ask them to park so you can't see the insurance logo. When Hanky or Detective Taylor calls, put them through to one of the insurance guys. Okay?" I said.

"Why?" Frank was sniffling louder.

"Just do it, Frank. You will not be arrested, and it will all work out if you do as I tell you," I said and hung up. Uh oh, I did it again. I didn't say goodbye.

"I called Hanky's cell and it went to voice mail. I tried Taylor's and he answered. I asked him if they found LB and Donna yet, and he said no. I said I thought they would be visiting Julia soon so if he wanted to question them, that might be a good time. I also told him about the insurance guys at the bed and breakfast interrogating Frank and they would be questioning Julia as soon as she got home. I filled him in on what I suspected of LB and Donna.

"Can you wait there until they show up?" Taylor asked me.

"Don't you guys have drones or something you can send over here to hang out and watch to see when LB shows?"

"Brandy, Brandy Alexander." Taylor was calling me by my first name twice since the night of the party. "You watch way too many TV cop shows," he said.

"Even kids have them now," I said.

"That's because kids have parents who can afford to buy them expensive things. NOPD barely has the money to pay us," he said.

"I'll wait. But you are going to give me a police escort, with flashing lights and sirens, so I can get around the rest of today in this traffic in order for me to finish my Christmas shopping," I said.

Taylor was laughing.

"I'm not joking," I said with all the dread in my voice I heard my mother use when we were kids.

"I'll escort you myself if this plays out like we anticipate," Taylor said and hung up.

Great, another one in need of phone etiquette training.

I started to text Julia to tell her to get home ASAP. I didn't really want to talk to her yet. None of this was going to make her happy. Before I hit send, she drove up the driveway going at least 50 mph and parked in the back where her car wasn't visible from the street.

I was parked out front and waited for LB to show up. I checked messages and sent some voice mails in case they came up on me without me noticing. I'd want to look like I was stuck in my car on the phone. I was parked on Canal Street at the corner of Julia's bed and breakfast facing the river. After a few minutes, Hanky and Taylor drove by me headed lake bound on the other side of Canal. In my rearview mirror I saw them turn right at the next corner. They had to make two more right turns at the next corners because then I saw them drive up the side street heading back to Canal Street. They parked on the other side of Canal Street at the corner. They were looking straight at Julia's front door and at me. They pulled in behind a car so no one would notice them. I got a text from Hanky that said, *In position. Hope you are right.*

We didn't wait long. LB drove up into Julia's side driveway and Donna Twilight was with him. I pulled in behind him.

When LB and Donna got out of the rental car, I noticed she had on new clothes and was toting two Saks Fifth Avenue shopping bags from Canal Place filled to the brim. Donna's clothing choices seem to have a constant theme, and no matter what she chose, it was skintight. Thank God they didn't make her wear that red jumpsuit home she had on the night of the party. Today she had on black stretch pants and a red sweater that dipped down her back to the waist. It, too, was body hugging.

"Hey, Brandy, you're blocking me in," LB said as soon as I opened my car door.

"Hey LB. Donna. I'm only running in to drop these off. I'm not staying," I said as I got out of the car holding two boxes of Kringles. "You both have to have a slice of this if you've never had Kringles. You are going to love me forever after you try one."

The three of us walked up the front steps and Julia answered the door. LB kept looking back over his shoulder at my car blocking him in.

"I'll be out of here in a flash," I said to him.

Julia opened the front door. "Where's Frank?" I asked her after we all did the cheek-to-cheek kiss exchange.

"Probably in the kitchen. He called me to say there's someone here to see me, so I asked him to have them wait in the double parlor," she said. "Are those Kringles? You know I love those, and you are gonna make me get fat." She turned to Donna and said, "Donna, you and I can only have a small piece. We single girls need to watch our figures." She turned back to me and said, "Brandy, would you take those to the kitchen for me please and give them to Frank."

Oh boy, was Julia laying it on thick. If I didn't know better, I would have made Julia and Donna out as BFFs.

"I'll just help Donna upstairs," LB said, looking at Julia in an odd way. "Julie, I told her you said it's all right if she stays here a few days, right baby?"

"Of course," Julia said. The way she was smiling, I imagined Julia was mentally licking her lips waiting to eat LB alive. "Go on, help Donna. I'll be in here a few more minutes and then I'll come up and see if she needs anything."

LB was about to help Donna upstairs even though she didn't look like she needed it. She sprinted up that flight of steps ahead of him with those two large shopping bags from Saks Fifth Avenue like it was an Olympic event. As soon as LB and Donna were upstairs, I texted Hanky and Taylor that it was clear to come in.

I went to find Frank to give him the Kringles.

"What's going on?" I asked Frank when I got to the kitchen. "What set this in motion?"

Frank was fanning himself with one hand while he said, "I called the insurance company like she asked me to, and the next thing I know, these two are here wanting to see the bracelet she wants added to the insurance policy. When I went to look for it, it's not in her jewelry box or the safe. They said from the photo I sent them, it matched a police report indicating it was stolen property."

"Relax, Frank," I said. "Everything is going to work out."

"If she didn't come home when she did, those two guys would have hauled me off in handcuffs and none of you would have ever seen or heard from me again," Frank wailed.

"This isn't China where you get shanghaied. The insurance people would have returned to ask Julia where the bracelet was," I said. "They want to find the bracelet so they don't have to pay the claim or they can recover what they paid. They will get the police involved if an arrest needs to be made."

I went back to where Julia waited at the front door for Hanky and Taylor.

A man and a woman dressed in dark business suits were standing in the double parlor. I opened the front doors to let Hanky and Taylor walk in without knocking.

Detective Taylor asked Julia, "Can you lock everything from this security panel here by the front door? Windows, front doors, back door?"

"Yes, and I already did. That sucker isn't going anywhere except with you."

Julia and I waited in the center hall while the police said they needed to talk to the insurance guys.

"What do you know?" I asked.

"I know this bracelet he gave me was one he stole from a woman he dated or was seeing in California. Her late husband had given it to her but he had insured it. The insurance company has been tracking him for over a year," she said. "Every time they got close, he moved or the woman he gave it to didn't realize it was missing for a few days. The lucky thing is the first woman had insured it or there would be no end to this hustle. I feel so stupid."

"Why, because some professional hustler said and did things to make you like him?" I asked. "How would you know; how would anybody? They know how to exploit our feelings within seconds of talking to us. This is on him, not you."

"I had asked Frank to call my insurance company and add the bracelet to the jewelry rider. I had him send a photo of it I took with my cell phone. That sent up a red flag and those two showed up here," she said, nodding to the two insurance people.

"I'm sorry," I said.

"I don't trust my judgment with men anymore," she said.

"This will turn out fine. So far he's into you with the bracelet," I said. "You're driving the bus right now."

"I was wearing the bracelet when they got here. I walked in and heard Frank saying,

'Why would I call you to insure something and let you come here if I knew it wasn't here. Someone has taken it or maybe Julia moved it.' He was in tears. When he saw me he got excited and looked a little relieved. I explained I asked him to call and add it to my policy," she said. "Then Detective Taylor called and told us what to do."

We could hear footsteps all over upstairs. It sounded like both LB and Donna were looking for something.

Y Y Y

WE WAITED A few minutes before LB came down the stairs. He told us Donna was still upstairs resting. Then he said, "This is so nice of you to let her stay here. I might have to ask you to extend your hospitality to me since my hotel is booked up with the holiday."

I thought, booked up for the holiday? The hotel business was dead in New Orleans over Christmas and picked up with New Year's parties a week later.

"Julie, think I can stay here a day or two, baby?"

Julie again, not Julia. If you're going to hustle someone at least call her by her correct name.

Before Julia could answer, he noticed the two people wearing dark suits sitting in the double parlor.

"Who's that?" he asked.

"Oh, they stopped by to get pricing and check availability for the group they are bringing here next month. I gave them a price sheet to review. I'll see if they have any questions before they leave," she said.

Detectives Hanky and Taylor walked around behind the staircase so LB didn't see them leave the double parlor until they stepped out of the dining room.

"Hello Detectives. How's it going? Have you found who killed my sweetheart's baby brother?" LB extended his hand to Taylor.

I had to give it to him. He was smooth.

Detective Taylor reached for his pen and notepad from inside his coat pocket while saying, "We have a couple of questions for you and Donna if you don't mind. It'll only take a minute."

"Sure," LB said. "I'll go get her." He started back up the stairs but Taylor grabbed him by the arm.

"We'll get to her after we talk with you," Taylor said as he pulled LB by the arm and guided him toward Julia's dining room with the double pocket doors.

"Just trying to help," LB said in his most-jovial manner.

Hanky said, "Let's talk in here where we have some privacy," and closed the double doors to the hallway.

Julia and I immediately went to listen at the space where the double doors met. There was a small crack where they didn't meet flush and I had a sliver of a view of Detective Taylor.

Hanky let Taylor take the lead questioning LB. He asked, "So, did you help Julia the day of the party around here?"

"Yeah, she had us all running around like chickens with our heads cut off," LB said.

"ALL? Who all was here?" Taylor asked.

"Well, me, Frank, and the guys outside setting up all that stuff on the lawn."

"So, you worked inside or outside?" Taylor asked.

"Well, both. I did what she asked me to do," LB said, confident in his answers.

"So, did you do any landscaping outside? You know, set up the decorations, trim some hedges, cut some flowers?" Taylor asked.

Now LB sounded cautious in his answer, but I had a feeling he knew where this was going. "Well, I only did what my Julie asked me to do. I cut some flowers for her. She asked me to go out and find some flowers for her table," he said.

I grabbed Julia by the arm discreetly and put my finger over her lips to keep her from blowing a gasket. I knew she wanted to scream out, "Liar, there are no flowers out there right now," because I wanted to scream at him too.

"So, you say Julia asked you to cut some flowers?" Taylor asked.

"Yes."

"Which ones?" Taylor asked without looking up and writing some notes.

"I don't know names of flowers, Detective. You gonna have to ask my Julie."

"Were they those big red flowers out there?" Taylor asked.

"No. I know those. Those are Christmas flowers. I think their name is point-setters," LB said. "No, not those."

"So, you know some flowers. You know it was not a poinsettia. Just tell me or show me which bush you cut flowers from," Hanky asked, waving a hand around like she wanted LB to point in the direction of the bush.

"Well, I cut them from the bush out there on the side of the house. It's under the parlor window," he said, pointing to the windows on the opposite side of the house. "Right under the third window from the front."

"What would you say if I told you that's an oleander bush?" Taylor asked.

"Maybe. Like I said, I don't know flowers," LB said, smiling feeling sure of himself.

"How many did you cut?" Taylor asked. "A big bunch of flowers or a small bunch?"

"I cut her a big old bunch of them flowers so she'd have enough for her dining room table," LB said.

"What did you do with the flowers you cut? Did you put them in vases?" Taylor asked.

"I gave them to Julie like she asked me to," he said.

"Where did she use them or put them?" Taylor was looking straight at him.

"I have no idea. I like flowers and all, but I don't see how this is helping find the killer," LB said. "All I did was cut some flowers she asked me to cut and I gave them to her. I don't know what she did with them after that."

"Mr. Sutton, what would you say if I told you Julia said you didn't cut any flowers?" Taylor asked and stopped writing notes.

"Well, maybe cuz I just set them down in the kitchen. I didn't actually give them to her, so I don't know what she did with them," LB said.

"Now you are saying you cut a big bunch of flowers and didn't give them to Julia but left them in the kitchen? What would you say if I told you we have a witness that saw you cutting branches off the oleander bush outside, and there were no flowers on that bush?" Taylor said putting his pen down and his tablet back into his coat pocket.

If I moved a little, I could see LB start to fidget with his bolo tie. "I'd say ask Julie why she wanted me to cut that bush and bring her the branches."

"Now you're saying she asked you to cut dead branches off that bush?" Taylor asked.

"I'm saying I did what Julie asked me to do," LB stammered.

Juli-A. With an A, not an E! I wanted to scream. Now he was trying to throw her under the bus without even using her proper name.

Taylor stayed cool. He said, "So now you're changing your statement to say Ms. Richard asked you to cut branches off what looks like a dead bush for her Christmas party? Is that right?"

"Yes. I don't know what she wanted them for," he said.

"Well, what would you say if I told you oleander turned up in the boxes of rum balls that Donna fed Larry?" Taylor said.

"If Donna fed them to Larry, maybe Donna cut them and put them in the rum balls," LB said.

"Mr. Sutton, we'd like for you to come downtown to answer some more questions," Detective Taylor said.

Just then there was a loud knock on the front door which made Julia and me jump almost as high as the second floor landing. Through the leaded glass doors, I could see two New Orleans policemen in uniforms. At the same time, the double doors opened and Hanky and Taylor walked LB out and handed him over to the uniforms. The uniforms started to handcuff LB.

LB started to protest and Detective Taylor said, "Oh, we're not arresting you for Larry Richard's murder…yet. These insurance guys have questions regarding jewelry, in particular the one on Ms. Richard's arm. We're assisting them in arresting you on that matter. There's the business of several jurisdictions around the country who want someone matching your exact description brought in for questioning. But, before we give them a crack at you, we'll talk to you about your conspiracy to murder Larry Richard." As Taylor ushered him out of the front door.

I heard him starting to read LB his Miranda rights.

The insurance people came out of the double parlor and the man followed Taylor out, but the woman stopped in front of Julia. Without saying a word, Julia took off the bracelet and handed it to her.

Detective Hanky asked Julia to tell Donna the police requested her to come downstairs.

"With pleasure," Julia said and almost sprinted up the steps. Nothing gets Julia moving like the thought of revenge.

Donna started to come downstairs and saw the flashing blue lights of the NOPD squad cars out front and Hanky waiting at the bottom of the stairs.

"Hello, Donna," Hanky said. "I just want to tie up a few loose ends. Have a minute?"

"Yeah, sure," she said, but she looked around behind her rubbing her hands up and down on her pants. She didn't sound real sure and she stood there.

"Let's go sit in here," Hanky said and waved an arm toward the sofa in the double parlor. "I just need to get your recollection on a couple of things the day Larry was poisoned."

Donna took her time coming down the staircase, holding on as if she needed the support for her recovery. She sat on the very edge of the sofa with her hands in her lap almost between her legs. Her back was ramrod straight, and she looked like she would bolt any second.

Hanky asked her, "Are you more comfortable with me calling you Donna or Cherie?"

"What? My name is…." she started to say but Hanky cut her off.

"We know who you are and what your real name, I mean, names are. Now, LB said you know how poisonous oleander is, having grown up in the area and the bushes are everywhere. Right?"

Donna looked from Hanky to Julia to me and back to Hanky. "I know what oleander looks like. I didn't know it was poisonous. Is it?"

"You know it is," Hanky said. "Would you be surprised to hear that LB said that you sprinkled the boxes of rum balls with the dried oleander leaves and used the twigs in the rum balls like toothpicks in order to poison Larry?" Hanky asked her, and Donna's eyes opened wide. I thought this might be the first time she ever had her eyes open during this entire ordeal.

"I bet you wouldn't be surprised to hear that LB said you cut the oleander twigs. He said you told him you could get Larry to eat anything you fed him, and it was your idea to use oleander as toothpicks to make sure they did the job, right?" Hanky asked. "In fact, you handled it too much, and Larry made you eat one of the rum balls that made you sick? I bet you didn't count on that."

"LB would never say such a thing," Donna said standing up.

"He would and he did. Now sit back down. We have a few more questions," Hanky said. "How long have you been Mrs. Sutton?"

Donna started to unravel. She was looking back and forth and squeezing her hands together. "LB wouldn't say that. He wouldn't blame me. He said we can't testify against one another. We're married."

"Just when did you get married?" Hanky asked. "Because just about a week ago you were married to Ms. Richard's brother, Larry Richard. Maybe you're a bigamist? Are you? Are you a bigamist? Because that's illegal."

"No, no, I'm not a bigamist. I married LB this morning at the courthouse here. It was after Larry died," she said.

"After Larry died and after you told LB about Larry's inheritance? Or did you tell him about that money before you married Larry?" Hanky was staring at Donna and not writing down anything.

"What?" Julia blurted out. Hanky and I both looked at her.

"Well, you weren't married to LB when you two decided to kill Larry," Hanky said. "That means that married thing where you don't think you can testify against each other doesn't matter. Besides, LB already told us it was you and that's why he's going downtown to give his full statement so we can clear him and he can go home."

"It wasn't my idea to poison your brother. It was all LB's idea," Donna wailed. "I…I…it was LB's idea to use oleander. He said he's used it before. He gave me the twigs and some crushed, dried leaves and said to roll anything Larry liked to eat in it. When he started on the rum balls, it was just easy to get him to use the twigs."

Julia looked like she was about to lunge for Donna's throat, so I grabbed her by the arm and pulled her into the center hallway. The last thing I heard was Donna asking Hanky if she was under arrest, and Hanky telling her the Miranda rights.

Chapter Eighteen

T HE OFFICE PARTIES were fun, especially since I managed to finish all the work necessary to keep my manager and, more importantly, my clients happy. My office had a serve yourself bar and trays of sandwiches and finger food delivered from Costco. Jiff's office party on Friday night had bartenders and servers walking around in black pants and white shirts with hot and cold canapés and hor'doeuvres on trays. It was a great party on the top floor of Canal Place in their suite of offices. There was a three-piece jazz band playing enjoyable music and not so loud that we couldn't speak to each other.

Jiff said, "I was going to ask Frank if he wanted to work the party. He's a good waiter."

"Did you forget Frank's wardrobe may not be what you had in mind for this sort of gala?" I asked. We both laughed. "But, you're right. He is a good waiter."

"I wanted to tell Julia I would be happy to look over any documents her dad's attorney sends her to open the succession," he said. "Pass that along to her, would you?"

"Yes, I will." I said. "I wanted to tell you, when Julia heard from those guys her brother worked with about how Larry wanted to help Donna and that he always had a soft spot for the broken ones, she wanted to contribute too. So, she decided to open a facility to help girls like Donna have options other than working in a bar. She's still working through the details, but she wants a place that helps young women to get a GED, learn some computer skills, and how to apply for better jobs. Frank can always help them dress for success."

"That's wonderful. I'll help her anyway I can," Jiff said. "So, how did you figure it was LB and Donna in cahoots?"

"After I spoke to Agnes, the president of the gourmet cooking club, and she was sharp, she told me she checked every box to make sure only rum balls were in it so that no member could give an unfair clue to vote on their entry. If the twigs weren't in the boxes and no one got sick except for Larry and Donna, then someone put the twigs in those boxes. I remembered Donna went and got the twigs out of a box when Larry went to a new box. There were a few things that alone didn't alarm me, but together they did."

"Like what?"

"Like, LB was in a hurry to get Donna to the ER the night they ate the poison. He didn't make much of an effort for Larry," I said. When I saw Jiff starting to protest, I added, "Ok, I know we all thought Larry was gone, but I think anyone else would have asked for help to get them both to the hospital. It struck me LB picked up Donna to get her help like she was his prized pet he had to save."

"I thought it was because she was still breathing," Jiff said.

"The other thing was LB was at the hospital with Donna way more than he was with Julia. Frank said he heard him snooping around upstairs. Then the guys in Houma said

Larry met Donna speed dating, and he didn't know what he had gotten himself tangled up with in her. I had Dante run LB's name and find out what businesses he owned. Guess what they were?"

"Bars that have speed dating?"

"Exactly," I said. "Guess what else he found?"

"The outstanding warrants for hustling women?"

"Right again." I said and kissed him. "LB and Donna didn't anticipate having Janice at her post, the kitchen window, and seeing LB cutting that bush. The timeframe made me keep asking what all happened to set everything in motion? It was Larry and Julia's dad dying and leaving all that money. That's a hard thing to keep quiet."

"I'm guessing Larry met Donna and she stayed close to him long enough to get him to marry her. Knowing Larry and how he wanted to help women, she found out or he told her he was coming into a lot of money," Jiff said. "That's hard for someone to keep a secret, especially someone who works hard every day of her life. She worked those bars in Texas for LB and probably told him Larry was a big fish. They weren't smart enough to look into Louisiana laws when it comes to wills, successions, and dying without a will," Jiff said.

"Yes. That's what Hanky and Taylor got out of those two after they questioned them. Each tried to pin it on the other one. You see, you figured it out too," I smiled and leaned in to kiss him.

"Let's go find my parents and make our plans for Christmas Eve," he said.

Both of Jiff's parents embraced me saying how happy they were that I was joining them for Christmas Eve. It was a tradition in their family to go to a Reveillon Dinner after midnight Mass at St. Louis Cathedral.

On the way home, Jiff told me his parents wanted us to come over to their home anytime after 7:00 p.m. They always serve a light party spread of food and later, after opening gifts, we would go to midnight Mass at St. Louis Cathedral. They had reservations for all of us at a restaurant serving a Reveillon Dinner following Mass in the French tradition. Most of the city, no matter your heritage, was happy to be influenced by the French culture.

I had never been to a dinner after midnight Mass. It was a French Creole tradition meaning awakening which celebrates the birth of Jesus. The French didn't stop celebrating after Mass. They went out to eat and drink to celebrate some more.

Since my family is Irish, we went home after church and ate the next day. Growing up Catholic we had to fast twenty-four hours before taking Communion. Now, that the fasting time has been reduced to one hour, most people eat, wait an hour, go to Mass and take Communion. My Irish mother wasn't about to start cooking after midnight, so we came home and she starved her children until Christmas Day.

When we got older and wanted to know why didn't we go to Reveillon Dinners after midnight Mass, the excuse she gave us when we no longer believed in Santa was she and my dad had to put together the toys for Santa to bring. We knew only my dad put together those toys. She was off to bed. My poor dad had to do that after midnight Mass at about 2:00 a.m., with no food. I see now why he insisted on leaving cookies and milk out for Santa. While our toys were put together in the morning when we woke, my French friends still had their toys in boxes to be assembled while their dads slept off a few glasses of wine with their late dinner.

I tuned back in to Jiff saying, "My dad's still trying to decide which restaurant he wants to go to. He's narrowed it down to Arnaud's, Antoine's, or Galatoire's, but my mother is worried he's waited too long to get a reservation."

"Your dad will have a reservation at whatever restaurant he decides on," I said.

"That's what my brothers and I have been telling her," he said. "My father and his firm has represented every kid (ever arrested or in trouble with the law) whose dad owns a restaurant in this city. They all owe him. In fact, there's a whole new generation of kids who now owe him. Right about now they are all praying he doesn't call them so they won't have to bump someone or squeeze in another table somewhere."

"I've never been to a Reveillon Dinner," I said. "This is a first for me."

"Great, our first Christmas together and our first Reveillon Dinner together with my family. I've never brought anyone to our family's Christmas Eve traditions. I didn't want to share it with anyone until I was sure," he said.

That made me nervous. As much as I wanted things ended with Dante, I was nervous about moving forward with Jiff and I still didn't know why. I was excited over spending Christmas Eve with him and his family, and glad I didn't have to sit with Dante's family and mine giving me the disapproving looks and tapping their watches to let me know it was time to set a wedding date. This year might be different since both my mother and Dante's mother were gaga over the idea of my sister having a baby, and one of Dante's brothers is the dad.

Dante was still his mother's favorite and she wasn't shy about telling everyone who would listen. His mother also wasn't shy at saying she wanted Dante to marry me. Yes, this was a good year to sit out Christmas as usual. That's what I had planned to do.

I WRAPPED MY last gift and it was to Jiff. There were a couple of different things I got for him. I marked the box, a thoughtful gift, that had a cashmere scarf to match his casual coat he wore with jeans in it. There was a fun gift which was a Sharper Image electronic radio he could ask to turn on and off with his voice. The last one was a romantic gift and it was a key to my apartment. He would know that I was ready to move on with him when he opened it.

It was a little after 5:00 p.m. and I was already dressed to go to Christmas Eve at Jiff's in the red silk suit he bought me that I had worn to Julia's ill fated party. I wanted to drop a couple of gifts off to friends and co-workers on my way uptown, and I wanted plenty of time so I could visit for a few minutes if asked to come in. I had fed Meaux who was going to accompany me this evening. He was wearing the plaid shirt-like vest I had for him with a small white collar and black bow tie. I also had a red scarf for his neck which matched the color of my suit.

Suzanne had already gone to her family's home for the evening. There was a knock on my front door and when I opened it, Woozie was on the other side of it, all dressed up in her new coat, hat, gloves, and shoes.

"Woozie, what are you doing here? Is something wrong?" I asked.

"Well, Merry Christmas to you too," she said. "Nuttin's wrong yet. I just worried you was not gonna see your dad like you promised."

"Come in. It's cold out there," I said, as she came in checking out the space I was renting. "Well, how did you get here?" I asked her stalling, for time to cough up a great excuse as to why I was not going to see my family this Christmas Eve.

"Uber. Your daddy set it all up. He know I only takes da bus. I don't know no Uber," she said. After looking me up and down, and there was never any way I could ever fib to Woozie, she added, "Humph. I knew it. You not plannin' to see yo' daddy. Is Woozie right?"

I let out a heavy sigh. "Yes, you're right. If I go see my dad, he is going to want me to go with him next door. Then Miss Ruth will cry if I say I can't stay. I don't want to start my Christmas Eve off with so much stress, and that's not even considering what my mother and sister can add. You know how they continue to derail things for me," I said. "Dante's not even going to be home, so I guess it isn't a bad idea to go if he isn't there. Don't look at me like that. I'll get you an Uber to go home."

"No. I'm not goin' home. You gotta take me over to yo' daddy's house. He made me promise and I keeps my promises. That's why I stopped here," she said.

"Oh, all right. I'll take you over there but I have about fifteen minutes of stuff left to do before I can leave. I told Jiff I'd meet him at his parents' house," I said. "I need to finish cleaning up Meaux's bowl and put the rest of this in the car."

If there was one person Woozie was more loyal to than me, it was my dad. She raised him and subsequently me, but he was her boy. I was a mere girl, so her loyalty to him trumped hers to me. I knew that. I just wished this thought had crossed my mind before I put her in my car and headed over to my parents' home.

Meaux sat in Woozie's lap on the drive to my parents' house. The two of them were comical in their new outfits. The plan was to bring him with me to Jiff's parents' so he could play with Isabella. Their housekeeper would let them both out since we would not be home until very late.

I hoped Mr. Albert wouldn't be coming home with the tree or that Miss Ruth wouldn't see my car and come over to beg me to visit even for a minute. I parked in front of my parents' house on the street so no one would block me in. The ground was cold and wet so I carried Meaux as we walked to the front door.

I asked Woozie, a little late on the uptake I might add, "Woozie why are you here at my parents' for Christmas Eve? You usually spend it with your family."

"Cuz yo' daddy asked me to make sure to get you here," she said as she knocked loudly on the front door three times, paused, and knocked two more times.

"Get me here for what?" I asked her. "Is that a secret knock?"

The door sprung open and my dad was standing there, grinning from ear to ear. He said, "Oh, good. You're here. Everyone is already next door. Let's go." He grabbed me and spun me around by the shoulders in a hug and ushered me along.

"Next door? No, no, no. I can't go next door. I have somewhere else I need to be," I tried to tell him but he was not having any of it.

He laughed a big old belly laugh, the laugh he had when he was up to something. This made me more nervous and apprehensive of what was going on. Woozie was in on it and fell in behind us, following us next door.

"Dad, wait a minute. I can't go over to the Deedlers. I have other plans," I said.

"Don't be silly. You are going to be so surprised," he said. "It's what you have been waiting for."

What have I been waiting for?

My stomach was so tight, it felt like the jaws of life were trying to pull it out through my belly button.

We were already at the Deedlers' front door. Dad knocked and it sprung open with both families all standing there looking at the three of us, four if you count Meaux. I stood there holding Meaux. My Dad was on my left with his arm still firmly gripping me around my shoulder, and Woozie was still standing to my right but a tad bit behind me. My dad was trying to take Meaux out of my arms, but I only held onto him tighter and tried to turned away from my dad. "Don't worry about a thing," he said. "I already gave Dante my blessing."

"Your blessing for what?" I asked right as I saw Dante come forward from the tribe of Deedler brothers surrounding him and get down on one knee as he opened a small, blue jewelry box.

I stood there mortified that my father all but dragged me next door after Woozie betrayed me by showing up unannounced at my place and asking for a ride to my parents' house.

The entire room was deadly quiet waiting for Dante to pop the big question and listening for my answer when Hanky stormed thru the front door announcing there was a multiple homicide with hostages and Captain Deedler was needed for it… NOW.

Dante looked relieved when he shoved the ring in his brother's hand and ran out the house behind Hanky like he was shot out of a cannon. I followed on their heels and jumped into my car. Dante had not officially asked the question, and I had not officially answered. I knew I never could.

My next call was to Jiff to tell him I was running a few minutes behind, but I was on my way.

The End

If you enjoyed this book, please consider giving me a review. I would greatly appreciate it and hope you look for my next book in the series.

Also, sign up for monthly newsletters and stories shared on the website, www.colleenmooney.com.

About the Author

Colleen Mooney was born and raised in New Orleans, Louisiana, where she lives with her husband and rescued schnauzers. She graduated from Loyola University of the South and has lived in Birmingham, Alabama, New York City, Madison, New Jersey and Atlanta, Georgia. She has been a volunteer for Schnauzer Rescue of Louisiana in the New Orleans area for over fourteen years and has placed over 350 abandoned, surrendered or stray schnauzers. If you are interested in learning more about New Orleans or have questions for Colleen, please contact her at one of the following:

email:

colleen@colleenmooney.com

Website:

www.colleenmooney.com

Facebook:

facebook.com/ColleenMooneyAuthor

Twitter:

twitter.com/mooney_colleen

OR

To find out more about Schnauzer Rescue visit their webpage, Facebook or email and share photos of your BFF with us here:

www.nolaschnauzer.com

facebook.com/NOLASchnauzerRescue

Email: nolaschnauzer@gmail.com

Dog Gone and Dead

From The New Orleans Go Cup Chronicles

THIS WAS WAY too early on a Saturday morning for any dog to go outside. It was still dark; the woman was half awake, so she didn't realize the leash didn't connect to his collar. She blamed herself for not hooking him to the leash before she picked him up and carried him across the highway to the beach side. She tried calling him a couple of times before she realized he was not paying attention and already had a good lead on her. The wind was blowing in her face so it was unlikely he could even hear her.

After wrapping the leash around her wrist like a bracelet, she took off running after him as fast as she could. *That Rascal,* she thought, *he lives up to his name.* As soon as she stood up thinking he was hooked to his leash, he broke free and headed toward the water. The sand was deep where the woman stood. Rascal was making more progress. Rascal had the advantage of four-paw drive, and he was running closer to the water's edge where there was firmer footing. She made her way over to the wet sand.

In the darkness Rascal was barely visible and the distance between them was expanding. The full moon reflected off the sand giving just enough light to spot him up ahead. He was having a gay ole time running as fast as he could. She'd never catch him if he kept up this pace. When she got closer to the pier she was afraid she would lose him for good. He would be out of sight for a few seconds. He might turn left and make his way to the parking lot and over to one of the neighborhoods across the highway.

Running along the wet packed sand made it easier to control her breathing and she picked up her pace thankful for a routine of morning runs. It was good training for chasing this guy along the beach. She wished he would stop and sniff something, and then she could catch up to him.

When she got to the pier, she didn't slow her pace. When she ran under it, something hit her hard on the back of the head. As she fell, stunned, she thought something tripped her. It was harder to see in the shadows under the pier. When she turned to see what it could be, someone stepped out from the darkness. Her last thought was *what would happen to her sister and little Rascal now if this guy got his hands on them.*

Chapter One

SUNRISE BROKE THE darkness in Jiff's family condo overlooking the Gulf of Mexico waking me up with its arrival. My boyfriend, Jiff Heinkel, and I both live in New Orleans. We were finally on a much-needed weekend alone. Even in late February, the weather was perfect, not too hot and not too cool. My name is Brandy Alexander, and I love the beach this time of year. We might get a cool snap, but it's normally very nice weather with no one around to share the beach with.

His condo was the penthouse, seventeen stories up on Gulf Boulevard, with a spectacular view of the Florida beach with its pure white sand and turquoise blue water. I couldn't wait to go for a swim. We had gone to bed leaving the sliding door open to listen to the soft sound of waves rushing onto the beach. It worked its magic as the sound carried up to our room with the sea air and lulled us to sleep.

While this was a family stretch of waterfront condos I always loved to come in the late winter or early spring before the families and college kids littered the sand. I find the beach is better enjoyed without music blasting. I could do without dodging volleyballs or footballs, tripping over water rafts, sand toys, and hearing the playful screaming that came along on family vacations.

I nudged Jiff and whispered in his ear, "C'mon, let's go for a walk before anyone else is up."

"No one else is up," he said, rolled over and put a pillow over his head. I heard a muffled, "What time is it?"

"Almost six-thirty," I said and pulled the pillow off his face so I could try to kiss him awake. It was really only six-o-five.

"We're on vacation. The beach will still be deserted at nine. No one goes out before noon," he grumbled and with his eyes still closed reached around for his pillow.

"I'll go by myself," I said, bouncing off the bed.

"Okay, just give me a sec," he said, but he laid there a few more minutes.

"I already have my suit on," I called from the bathroom. I combed my shoulder length, blonde hair and pulled it up in a ponytail. I stepped into a black, one-piece bathing suit that only covered what a bikini should cover and the rest of the suit had mesh holding it together. I took a second to admire the hours I had put in at the gym all winter and I was pleased with the results. I added a black and white cloth hat that had a floppy look about it. It could roll up and be stuck under a shoulder strap if I got tired of wearing it.

"Here," I said throwing his swim trunks on the bed. "You don't even need to get up to get dressed. C'mon. It's beautiful out there right now. Just you, me and the beach."

When we made it to the sand, Jiff was still walking like a Zombie. Going through the loose, deep sand I thought he looked a little tipsy since he wasn't fully awake until I realized he had his eyes shut.

"Even with my eyes closed, I can tell we are on the beach," he said. "I feel sand between my toes." He removed his sunglasses and rubbed his eyes for the umpteenth time.

"I thought you might be sleep walking because you haven't said anything about my new suit. I bought it just for this trip," I said. "You know I love the beach."

Jiff made an effort to open both eyes wide. He looked me up and down taking in my new bathing suit and said, "I know you love the beach. And I love you."

Wait. What? This was the first time he said I love you. It felt as though something sucked the air off the entire beach. I didn't want to make too much out of it or too little. I casually added, "I love you, too."

He scooped me up off my feet and spun around. He was fully awake now. When he set my feet back in the sand he said, "I'll race you to the pier," and took off running.

"Oh, you've been playing me, you big cheater!" I yelled at his back.

I was never going to catch him since he had too much of a lead and a much longer stride. He also had run track in high school and college while I had run my mouth. I saw him ahead of me. He stopped sharply and turned away from the water's edge under the pier. He stood looking down at something. Something that looked like a beach towel or blanket all balled up.

When I approached, Jiff turned and said, "No, don't come closer. This is bad."

"What? What is it?" Leaning around him I managed to get a look at the top part of the girl that was on the sand and half floating in the water. "Oh, no. That poor girl. Did she drown?"

"I'm not sure, but from the look of her, I don't think she's been in the water. I see bruising around her neck. We need to call the police," Jiff said looking up and down the beach to see if there was anyone else around.

"We left our cell phones in the room."

"Yeah. Look, walk back away in your own footprints in the sand so we don't contaminate this crime scene any more than we already have," Jiff said. He was an attorney in his dad's criminal law practice and had defended a friend of mine in the past.

"I'll stay here and make sure no one else walks up on her," I said trying to see what was wrapped around her wrist.

"No, I'll stay here and you run up to the street and see if you can find a phone or someone with a phone. I don't want you alone if someone is still lurking about," Jiff said.

"Okay," I said and squatted down to get a better look at what was wrapped around her wrist. It was a dog's leash wound partially around the woman's arm with the end floating in the water lapping at her side. "Look, she must have been walking her dog, but where's the dog?" I could feel Jiff getting ready to react to my being so close to the woman. I held up my hand and added, "I'm not going to touch anything."

"I don't want to move her. The local police will love that but she might be floating away soon and the water might destroy evidence," he said.

Before I stood up, I looked up and down the beach and said, "I think it's safe to say she lost Rascal and Rascal is a Schnauzer."

"Rascal? How do you know he's a Schnauzer?" he asked looking up and down the beach mimicking me.

Schnauzers were our thing. Well, it was definitely my thing. I rescued them and found homes for those people had abandoned or left at shelters. I had one and Jiff had one. He saw me bringing a rescue to a man in his condo complex and shortly after that we had a chance meeting and started dating. It sounds simple, but like Tina Turner… I never do anything nice and easy, not even when it came to meeting the man of my dreams.

I pointed to the part of the leash that had unwound from her wrist. It showed an image of a little salt and pepper schnauzer stitched right in front of RASC. "I'm guessing that's the first part of the dog's name on this leash," I said. "It's one your special-order sets with the dog's name and a picture of the breed on it. Sometimes the collar has the owner's phone number stitched into it like the name is on the leash." I started to point closely to one section on the woman's wrist. "Look right here…"

"Don't touch it." Jiff said it so loud I jumped. "Sorry."

"Give me some credit, please." I had picked us a small thin piece of driftwood. Using it I lifted the part of the fabric floating in the water so he could see the part I could see still on her wrist. "There's a Schnauzer image stitched right next to the name. I'm guessing the name is Rascal. I was going to order my Meaux and your Isabella one for next Christmas."

I carefully walked in my own footsteps back up the beach while Jiff took a couple of steps back and yelled, "I'll wait here and keep anyone else from walking up on her, but don't let anyone see you in that swim suit."

I looked at him, shook my head, shrugged my shoulders up asking him, "So do you think I should take it off to go look for a phone?"

“I wish I had put on a T-shirt,” he said.

Chapter Two

THE ONLY PLACE I found open at six-twenty-five a.m., was a Tom Thumb Gas Station and Convenience Store across the street from the fishing pier. I felt exposed with no beach cover-up over my suit but it did get the attention of the clerk behind the counter. He let me use the phone to call the police. I'm not even sure he heard me say I found a dead woman under the pier.

By the time I got back to Jiff, two uniformed police officers were already there marking off the area with crime scene tape. A barefoot guy, with BEACH PATROL written in large yellow lettering across the back of his very tight, black, neoprene shirt, was helping them.

Jiff was standing back away from the area where they were working near the dune buggy I assumed the Beach Patrol dude arrived on.

"Did you ask Surfer Boy over there," I said nodding to the shaggy haired guy wearing the beach patrol billboard, "if he saw a Schnauzer running loose?"

"No. I didn't. I think Surfer Boy is some sort of auxiliary cop. I think that's a gun under those beach jams. He came screaming up on that thing so I'm sure he thought I was his prime suspect. I told him what we found, and that you went to call the police leaving me to keep anyone from disturbing the crime scene. He called it in on his radio. The two uniforms were here in under a minute." Jiff said.

"I was probably still looking for a phone. This is a little different from trying to help the police in New Orleans, huh?" I asked him when we were downwind from the three of them.

"Yes, the two in uniform thanked me and said they were grateful I stayed to keep anyone from touching the body after we found it," he said. "They are very efficient, and polite. Surfer Boy seems a little full of himself."

"Even growing up next door to Dante didn't get me polite, let alone preferential, treatment. Since the holidays, I'm not sure there isn't some trumped up warrant out for my arrest," I said trying to be funny, but Jiff looked serious.

"Now that you mention it, I'll check to see if he has any outstanding warrants filed on you when we get back," he said and kissed my forehead.

My once, almost fiancé is now Captain Dante Deedler in the New Orleans Police Department. We have been permanently estranged since Christmas Eve. This is all due to the covert efforts of family members meddling in my life. Even our family housekeeper plotted against me. They all conspired and got me to his home on Christmas Eve so he could propose in front of everyone. This is after I had not seen or heard from Dante in weeks. It wasn't because he was in Iraq or somewhere fighting a war. No-o-o-o-o-o, he was downtown, about four miles away, working every day until he left for Houston for a three-day conference right before Christmas.

When he finally called from the conference a day before Christmas Eve—he told me it would be a good idea if I made other plans for the holidays. He didn't think he'd get a flight back to New Orleans for a few more days. The call was brief. He hung up on me before I could tell him I had been making other plans without him since—before Thanksgiving—the last time I had not heard from him.

Woozie, my parent's housekeeper, tricked me when she showed up unannounced at my apartment and asked for a ride to my parents' house. When I got there I had been mortified by my father who all but dragged me next door. Then Dante got down on one knee and shoved a blue ring box in my face. His entire family along with mine sat in the front row seats.

While I stood there stunned, knowing Jiff was waiting for me at his families' home, I waited for Dante to ask the question. Everyone waited for me to answer. The question never came.

I was saved when Detective Hanky, Dante's previous partner, stormed through the front door announcing there were multiple homicides in progress with hostages, and Captain Deedler was needed for it...now.

Dante looked relieved when he shoved the ring in his brother's hand and ran out the house behind Hanky like he was shot out of a cannon. I followed on their heels. Had it not been for a multiple homicide that could have been my worst Christmas ever.

The two Navarre Beach police officers were staring at me waiting for an answer while I was daydreaming about the last holidays. Jiff nudged me back to the present. They had asked our names and how to reach us and took our statements. I informed the female officer taking my name and information that it appeared the lost dog was a Schnauzer, based on the special order leash embroidered with the name and breed on the dead woman's wrist.

"I do Schnauzer Rescue in New Orleans. You can Google me or find our Facebook page. Here's the number for Homicide Detective Hanky with the NOPD who will vouch for me, well, vouch for us," I said, nodded toward Jiff. I wrote Hanky's cell phone number on her notepad.

"I'll give her a call," Officer B. Frederick responded without looking up.

"Detective Hanky adopted a dog from me and I think of her as a friend. I think she still holds it against me that I date this guy," I nodded toward Jiff speaking with the other officer. "Detective Hanky is the former partner to my ex-boyfriend who is now her Captain."

"Ouch, bet that was tough. One cop in a relationship is one too many," Officer B. Frederick said without a smile, like she might be speaking from experience. There was no wedding band on her finger and she looked to be forty-something.

"So, if you find the little dog, I'd be happy to take him and try to find him a good home," I said. I told her how to find me on the internet under my non-profit rescue site and wrote down my name and number after Hanky's information on her notepad.

"Hey Bev, give her the name of the local shelter here. They might hold him a week or so if anyone brings him in," the male officer suggested. His name tag read J. Davis, and he looked half of Bev's age.

Officer "Bev" Frederick wrote the name and address of the shelter on a page in her notebook, tore it out, and handed it to me.

"If someone finds him along the beach here, it's likely they might take him home. Most of the visitors along here are from out of town," she said closing her notebook.

"Whoever finds him, I just hope they love him and take care of him," I said. "Most people consider them high maintenance because they need regular grooming about every six weeks that costs about forty to forty-five bucks."

"I'll pass that along if I hear if anyone has found him or is considering keeping him. I'll give them your number to talk to, if that's okay?" she asked.

"Sure. I'm happy to help any way I can. I would hope someone would do it for me if my dog was lost," I said. I took a last look at the dead woman before the younger male officer started covering her up.

Beach Patrol, whose name "Magic Mike" was embroidered on the front of his skin-tight shirt, looked like he was about to jump in his dune buggy and ride off into what was left of the morning mist. Instead, he made his way over to us and asked our names and where we were staying.

"My name is Brandy Alexander and I'm, well we're both from New Orleans. We're here for a long weekend," I said. "We plan to leave Monday."

"Brandy Alexander, huh? From New Orleans, well that makes sense," he said without smiling. "What's your boyfriend's name, Jim Beam?"

"No, Jack Daniels. So, you're Magic Mike?" I asked.

"Hey, look, just trying to get the basics here," he said.

"My name is Jiff Heinkel and I'm a criminal defense attorney in New Orleans," Jiff said and reached to take my hand. "We're staying at the Beach Breeze Condos, number 101."

I added with the nicest voice I could, "Would you look for the Schnauzer? I think it belonged on the end of that leash the dead woman has around her wrist. I do breed rescue for them and I'll find him a good home."

Neither Jiff nor I had anything to write with so Magic Mike pulled one of his cards from a side pocket of his baggy, knee-length shorts, an odd choice I thought with the skin-tight top. The card was laminated with just his name and phone number on it. I bet he gave these to all the girls.

"Text your info to that number and I'll call you if I find him," he said.

"He might have a collar on with the name Rascal on it," I said. "See," I pointed to the leash floating in the water just inches away from where the body remained covered. "They are a custom set people order for their pets."

"Cool," he said without looking at the leash on the woman's arm I pointed to. "I'll call you if I find him." Then he revved his ride and took off leaving the uniform police to wait for forensics, the coroner, and the crime scene investigating personnel.

"Dune buggies…riding lawnmowers with a sun roof," Jiff said more to himself than to me.

He took my hand and pulled me along back to our condo.

"You thought there wouldn't be anyone on the beach till noon," I said. "We met three new people and did a good deed finding that girl before she floated away. Maybe we'll do another and find her dog."

"Yes, and if we waited around any longer, we'd be stuck there all morning," he said. "They know where to find us. Not exactly the way I wanted to start our long weekend."

"Me neither, but I'm worried about that little dog. I'd really like to find him."

"C'mon, Brandy, I know you. You want to solve this murder and find out who killed her."

"No. I don't need to find her killer. I want to find that dog, but… if I find out who killed her along the way, well, that would be the bonus round."

"This is supposed to be a relaxing trip," Jiff said with an emphasis on 'relaxing'.

"I'm relaxing," I said. "Let's go for a ride up the beach and then we can come back and I'll make you breakfast."

"A ride up the beach?" Jiff asked. He stopped and looked at me. "You're not fooling me. You want to ride up the beach and look for that dog, don't you?"

"Well… yes, but, only for an hour or so, then I'll be satisfied."

"You won't be satisfied until we find him," Jiff said shaking his head. "I have a sunset sailing trip scheduled for six o'clock this evening," he said looking at his watch.

"Oh, we'll be back way before then," I said waving my hand at him like it was no big deal.

He let out an exaggerated breath.

"You can't be tired already," I teased. "Look, it's only seven-thirty a.m. and we've already had an adventure."

"All right. After our sunset sail this evening, I planned for us to have dinner down there on the beach. The sailboat is at a marina near Pensacola so I thought we could have dinner at the Grand Marlin. I made a reservation for eight-thirty if that's all right with you?"

"That is perfect. All I have to do today is make a phone call," I said.

"A phone call? To who?" Jiff looked at me sideways wrinkling his forehead.

"The animal shelter to give them my name and tell them I think there's a runaway Schnauzer that might be coming their way," I said.

He just shook his head as we made our way along the water's edge heading back toward our condo.

"When we found her, I noticed her footprints in the sand near the body. If they were hers, it seemed she was walking or running toward Fort Walton. Did you see that?" I asked trying to sound as casual as I could.

"No, I didn't notice her footprints," he said.

We walked along in silence while I churned details over in my head. Things I saw on the woman's body that might give me a hint as to where she stayed or where the dog might be headed. She was wearing running shorts, a T-shirt and rubber shoes sold at a sporting goods store to walk in the sand and water.

"I wonder why the dog wasn't leashed," I mused more to myself.

"No, I didn't see her footprints." he said again with a little too much emphasis on 'her'.

"Well, what did you see?" I asked. I knew he was messing with me now. He saw or noticed something while I went off on the 911 scavenger hunt.

"Paw prints. I saw small, paw prints that looked like they were running in the opposite direction we're walking now. The tide is coming in, so they're lost but it looked like the little bugger ran that way," he said. He turned around and held his arm out pointing straight ahead.

"I can't believe you. Why didn't you tell me this sooner? This little dog might be picked up on the highway and God only knows where he could wind up. I'm always afraid someone will use them as a bait dog in a dog fighting ring. We need to find him."

"Okay, let's go get the car keys and drive around for a few minutes. Maybe we'll spot him if he made it up to the highway before a car hits him."

"Are you trying to make me crazy?" I asked.